Tales from the Himalayas

Priyanka Pradhan has been a journalist since 2006, having reported on business news television channels in Mumbai (CNBC and Economic Times Now) and has written for newspapers and magazines such as *The Economic Times* and *Bloomberg Businessweek*.

She also covered travel and lifestyle for several international magazines such as *The New York Times Style Magazine* (UAE and Qatar editions), *Conde Nast Traveller*, (India and Middle East editions), *Harper's Bazaar* (Middle East), *Sorbet Magazine* (Europe) and *DestinAsian Magazine* (Indonesia), among others.

She is the recipient of the 'Ruskin Bond Promising Writer Award 2019' at the Dehradun Literature Festival, held in October 2019. She was also runner-up for the Montegrappa Writing Prize 2020 at the Emirates Literature Festival in the UAE, for a short story called, 'Postcard', which is part of this book.

Praise for the Book

Tales from the Himalayas has that unique storytelling quality that can transport you immediately into another world, where the wanderer's heart and soul truly desires to reside. It is at once an entertaining, heart-warming and delightful read for children and adults alike. Themes of family, belonging, loss, wonder and nature dominate the pages. It is the perfect escape from mundane city life and the urban burden. Even the re-read of the same story is as pleasurable as the first read.

Freida Pinto, actor

Tales from the Himalayas

Priyanka Pradhan

Published by
Rupa Publications India Pvt. Ltd 2020
7/16, Ansari Road, Daryaganj
New Delhi 110002

Sales centres:
Bengaluru Chennai
Hyderabad Jaipur Kathmandu
Kolkata Mumbai Prayagraj

Copyright © Priyanka Pradhan 2020
Book illustrations: Mohit Suneja

This is a work of fiction. Names, characters, places and incidents
are either the product of the author's imagination or are
used fictitiously and any resemblance to any actual person,
living or dead, events or locales is entirely coincidental.

All rights reserved.

No part of this publication may be reproduced, transmitted,
or stored in a retrieval system, in any form or by any means,
electronic, mechanical, photocopying, recording or otherwise,
without the prior permission of the publisher.

P-ISBN: 978-93-9035-670-6
E-ISBN: 978-93-9035-671-7

Sixth impression 2025

10 9 8 7 6

The moral right of the authors has been asserted.

Printed in India

This book is sold subject to the condition that it shall not,
by way of trade or otherwise, be lent, resold, hired out, or otherwise
circulated, without the publisher's prior consent, in any form of

To Ama, my favourite storyteller

Contents

1. The Bagpiper — 1
2. Daak Ghar — 10
3. The Great Himalayan Explorer — 22
4. The Snow Leopard — 28
5. Mischievous Teeth — 37
6. The Villain — 43
7. The Long-Lost Friends — 52
8. The Biggest Gift — 62
9. Chipko! — 69
10. The Village Monster — 80
11. The Spring Song — 93
12. Haria's Kitchen — 100
13. Kafal — 113
14. A Night in the Dark Forest — 120
15. Holi — 128
16. Pilgrimage — 138
17. Postcard — 147

1
The Bagpiper

'What makes a bagpipe sound good?' asked little Paru, while sitting in a wood workshop full of musical instruments.

Her father was holding his bagpipe in his hands. He had removed the wooden mouthpiece and was squinting one eye to look inside the pipe.

'Well, I have been playing the instrument since childhood and I can tell you one thing for certain,' he said.

'It is not the quality or age of the wood, nor the craftsmanship in making the instrument; it is not the softness of this leather bag, not even the talent of the bagpiper that makes this masak been (a type of bagpipe found in Northern India) sound beautiful.'

'Then what is it?' asked Paru, intrigued. She always liked the name masak been, because of the way Father said it.

'It is this,' he said, thumping his ribcage with a loose fist. 'Your heart, little girl,' he smiled. 'You must play from the bottom of your heart; only then will it sound any good.'

Paru and her father were looking for the perfect wooden mouthpiece for his bagpipe. Father needed a new one for his upcoming performance at a wedding procession in town. He often played the masak been at weddings and religious processions and was highly respected for his craft.

On her tenth birthday, Paru began her own bagpiping lessons under her father's expert tutelage. He encouraged her even though girls didn't traditionally play the bagpipe in the community. In fact, she was the only girl in the entire town who had shown interest in playing the instrument.

Every morning, she would wake up excited to begin the day's lessons.

The sound of hundreds of birds going about their daily business, the fresh smell of pine trees and the morning mist vanishing slowly to reveal the snowy peaks of the Himalayas was part of her bagpipe lessons. She always imagined that the birds sang to accompany her music, so she didn't mind being part of nature's concert, even at the break of dawn.

She practised every day, learning to play local tunes with her father, but she also liked to make up her own tunes. She jotted down notes for her own songs in a small notebook, hoping to surprise Father someday.

Then one day, there was wonderful news. A travelling fair had come to their town and was looking for local performers. It was an excellent opportunity to show off her talent, she thought.

'Are you sure, child? Why do you want to perform there?' Father asked, surprised when she asked him if she could participate.

'Father, I have worked so hard every day. The fair is

huge; there will be a big audience. I can't wait to perform and show my skills to the world!' she exclaimed.

Father laughed, 'I didn't know you were so keen to perform in front of an audience already!'

'But remember one thing, little one,' his tone became serious. 'Your talent is meant for your enjoyment, first. Don't play just for other people's appreciation; instead, enjoy the music yourself, regardless of how others respond.'

Paru did not understand what he meant. She didn't want to argue because it was getting late and she needed to wake up early next morning to travel to the big fair with Father.

As soon as the sun rose the next day, she wore her best outfit, polished her bagpipe until it sparkled and hopped on to the bus along with her father.

Outside the main gate, there was a desk set up to register participants. As her father jotted down her name in a form, she joined a long queue of performers, some older than her and some younger.

Suddenly, she felt a twinge of nervousness. She felt like someone had tied a big knot in her stomach.

She took a peek inside the main tent to see how many people had turned up in the audience and the knot in her stomach tightened even more. A sea of unknown faces was waiting to judge her performance. It looked like there were more than a hundred people there!

Her hands were now sweaty, and her face had lost all its colour. She knew her father would be sitting in the audience too, but that thought didn't console her. She was terribly frightened of the crowd.

When it was her turn, she managed to walk over to the centre of the stage, clutching her bagpipe tightly. There were murmurs in the crowd as she stood there in silence. The sights and sounds merged together and Paru could hear people giggling.

'They are laughing at me,' she realized. She managed to put her mouth to the instrument but to her horror, there was no sound.

The crowd jeered and there was more laughter.

She tried again and this time, the bagpipe emitted a loud belch-like sound. She couldn't believe it. Her bagpipe had just burped!

The crowd was now laughing outrageously, but she couldn't see anyone because her eyes had filled with tears. She ran offstage and kept running blindly, without knowing where she was going until her father caught hold of her. He hugged her tightly and said, 'It is okay, my love.'

She didn't speak a word on the bus back home.

The next day, she went up to her father and handed him her bagpipe. 'I am never doing this again,' she said, in a small voice. 'I'll never play again. Ever.'

Father simply nodded. 'I won't ask you to practise if your heart is not in it, but I know you'll play again,' he said.

She didn't believe him.

As months went by, Paru became a recluse. She didn't want to play with her friends because they had all heard about what had happened at the fair.

'The burping bagpiper!' they teased her whenever they

saw her. She was so embarrassed that she found it easier to avoid everyone rather than face the teasing.

Then one night, her father came home looking tired and crestfallen.

'Is everything all right, Father?' she asked, worried.

'Yes, my little one. Don't worry,' Father assured her. But later that night, she overheard him speaking with their neighbour.

'It's falling apart, Khemu. It's all falling apart,' she heard him say.

'Business is tough and it's getting worse by the day. Even the upcoming wedding at the main square next week has cancelled my performance. If things don't look up soon, I'll have to sell this house.'

'Oh dear, why is this happening?' asked Manu, the neighbour.

'I guess people find the bagpipe too traditional. Especially at weddings, nobody wants an old man playing the wailing bagpipe. I guess I am outdated,' Father sighed.

Paru was stunned. She couldn't believe that such a talented man was out of business. She wanted to help but didn't know how.

Suddenly, she remembered something and ran to her room. She grabbed a tin box and pulled it from under her bed and pulled out her old notebook.

'My notes for the songs I composed,' she whispered. 'Maybe they can work.' But she needed to practise them before presenting them to Father.

For the next six days, Paru practised her own

compositions day and night until they were near perfect. On the sixth night, she went up to Father's room to present the songs to him—they were peppy, new and original—nobody had heard them before. She hoped that he wouldn't be considered outdated if he played them.

But as she approached his room, she saw her father slumped in his chair, wiping his bagpipe clean, his shoulders drooping, and his eyes lowered.

Paru had never seen her father this disheartened before. That night, she tossed and turned but couldn't sleep. She had to come up with something to do; she simply couldn't bear to see her father like this.

The next morning, she packed a big cloth bag and started the steep ascent uphill to the main marketplace.

As she approached the top of the hill, a group of children passing by started to giggle when they saw her.

'The girl whose bagpipe burped at the town fair,' someone murmured, as they all burst out laughing.

She felt her cheeks flush as she stopped in her tracks, turned around and called out to those children.

'Actually, I can burp better even without the bagpipe and it goes something like this!' she said as she swallowed three large gulps of air and let out the loudest burp they had ever heard in their lives.

All she could do was laugh at their stunned faces, wave goodbye and resume her climb.

She couldn't believe how good that had felt—not caring about what they thought of her.

She didn't care that they all knew her performance was

a disaster anymore. All she cared about was reaching the top of that mountain and carrying out her secret mission.

When she finally reached her destination, she followed the crowd going towards the big wedding at the market square. It was the same wedding that her father was supposed to perform at before they cancelled it.

Buses full of guests were pouring in from all directions. The wedding was about to begin.

There were possibly more than 300 guests, which made it easier for little Paru to sneak inside the gate without being caught.

She waited and watched patiently as the wedding procession began. The bride in her beautiful spotted orange-and-yellow pichora (a traditional dress of women in Uttarakhand) made an appearance, and the pheras (a wedding ritual) took place.

Just as the wedding was wrapping up, Paru sprang to her feet, opened the big cloth bag and took her old, faithful masak been out of it.

As soon as the bride and groom stepped off the centre of the stage, Paru scrambled on top, and faced the crowd. There were hundreds and hundreds of people—a much bigger gathering than the crowd at the town fair. Her heart started thumping wildly again.

Palms sweaty, breath short and mind racing, for a moment she panicked. People turned to look, wondering who she was and what was she up to.

Paru closed her eyes. She remembered her daily early morning practice, the sounds of birds that accompanied her music and Father's voice saying, 'Go on, little girl. Play from your heart.'

And she did.

She played the songs she composed herself, and she played them with all her heart. She played with her eyes closed and her mind in deep meditation.

The audience was mesmerized by the little girl's incredible talent.

When she finally opened her eyes, she was met with the sound of deafening applause–people were on their feet, clapping and cheering for her.

She had finally done it.

The next day, her father answered the door to see a large group of people talking excitedly amongst each other.

'You are her father!' said one of them. 'Could you please give bagpiping lessons to my daughter too?'

'I need you to perform at our family procession next week. Please tell me you have the time!' exclaimed another.

'And for my brother's wedding next month,' said another.

Father was astonished.

'But...but how? Who? When?' he uttered, confused.

He looked at his daughter who was standing in a corner, to ask if she had anything to do with this.

She simply shrugged while turning her little hand into a loose fist and thumping at her ribcage. 'It is all from the heart,' she whispered, smiling.

2.
Daak Ghar

It was as if a giant dark cloud had descended upon the quaint town of Mukteshwar.

A traveller, who had just escaped a dreadful fate in the neighbouring forest, had come with a terrifying story. He had come sprinting out of the woods screaming when some villagers managed to calm him down and have him sit down for a drink of water.

He didn't speak the local language, but everyone could see from his wild, bloodshot eyes that something had shocked him out of his wits.

Through his gestures and animated demeanour, the villagers gathered that he had come from a dilapidated post office in the adjoining forest, not far from the village.

'Daak ghar, DAAK GHAR,' said the traveller. That's all they could understand.

'Letter! Letter!' he said next, shaking his head so vigorously that the villagers thought he was possessed.

The villagers nodded their heads as they knew there

were many abandoned post offices or 'daak ghars' in the forest. These post offices had been used by British officials during colonial rule but after India's independence, these houses were left unattended and had been in ruin for years.

From what the villagers could glean, the traveller had made the mistake of taking a break at the abandoned post office bungalow. He thought the bungalow was deserted, so he made himself comfortable on the porch and fell asleep till dusk. Suddenly, he awoke to high-pitched screeches that were coming from somewhere far but were getting closer by the minute.

'EEEHHHHHHHHHHH, EEEEEEHHHHH', the traveller attempted to mimic the sound.

He had figured something was amiss and had grabbed his bag to leave, but to his horror, he found he couldn't move. He must have fainted because the next thing he knew, he was lying in a massive pit, as if about to be buried alive. There were what seemed like human bones scattered all around. He managed to scramble out of the pit and ran for his life, not looking back.

The villagers listened, both mesmerized and terrified.

They knew this bungalow existed, but no one had ever been able to find it. Rumour had it that this cursed bungalow was invisible by day, and only appeared on full moon nights. Blood-thirsty ghouls, living in it, preyed on innocent passers-by and left them to die.

Amongst the villagers gathered around the traveller were four very keen listeners—siblings, Renu and Hari, and their friends, Aru and Manu, all from the village orphanage.

They huddled together immediately after the traveller had left and the crowd had dispersed. Thunder roared over them and lightning created terrifying shapes in the sky.

Renu thought the lightning looked like the fingers of a deadly witch, perhaps a premonition about the cursed daak ghar.

'It's about to pour heavily. Let's hurry,' said Renu to her brother Hari.

'Ha! You scared little rats,' laughed Aru. 'You have no guts.'

'It's not about guts, Aru. It's about being sensible. Look, a storm is brewing,' Renu tried to reason with him.

'If you want to prove you have any courage at all, come to the daak ghar,' Aru said, suddenly serious.

Manu and Hari looked at each other. They were scared but didn't want to admit it.

'Are you boys coming? Or are you also scaredy-cats?' asked Aru, menacingly.

'But what will we do there?' Manu asked.

'Oh we'll just have a look and investigate. Maybe this traveller is just a crazy man. Maybe he's just making up all these stories! Or perhaps it's true! Are you not curious to see what it's like?' Aru asked his friends.

In truth, they all were.

Aru gestured for them to follow.

'What, right now?' asked Renu, alarmed.

'Yes. Why? Is the little girl about to cry?' he laughed cruelly.

Despite herself, Renu found herself accompanying the boys on this lunatic mission.

It hadn't started raining yet and the black clouds blocked the moonlight completely. The group was left to navigate their way in darkness. Only the occasional lightning illuminated their path in bright fluorescent flashes, disappearing within seconds.

The thunder was so loud that it drowned the sounds of their own footsteps. The four friends had to hold each other's hands as they made their way through the forest.

After more than an hour of wading through the thicket around their village, they arrived at a large clearing in the woods.

Stepping lightly, the quartet made its way towards a large shadowy structure. There it was, hiding behind a thicket of deodar trees—the infamous daak ghar. The children gasped as three flashes of lightning sparked three separate parts of the house in a matter of a few seconds.

A broken staircase, on the right-hand side of the house, was cracked and blackened, a few brick-bare walls at the entrance had creepers coming out of their large crevices and massive broken wooden beams were hanging from the ceiling, swinging wildly in the strong wind.

There was no light inside, so the four had to make do with the light of a tiny torch that Aru had brought along.

Despite the foreboding atmosphere, they inched forward towards the main door.

Another quick flash of lightning illuminated the porch brightly, just enough for Renu to notice the massive front door creak open on its own. Nobody had touched it yet.

She didn't say anything, thinking it was the wind. But

she did feel goosebumps on her skin.

Aru stepped forward to push the door open, only to stare into darkness. They stepped over dried leaves that made rustling sounds and made their way into the house. Hari thought his foot hit something hard, so he bent down to inspect what it could be. Aru gave him the torch.

As Hari picked up the large, hard thing in his hand and pointed the torch at it, he froze. A chill ran down their spines as they realized he was holding a rib bone in his hand.

He screamed and dropped the bone, while Manu and Aru tried to calm him down.

'Shhhhhh,' said Manu. 'It could be the bone of an animal. One finds such things in the forest. Just be quiet.'

Renu could tell her brother was unnerved. She squeezed his hand to reassure him.

As they wandered about in the damp darkness, they saw cupboards, desks and chairs, broken and strewn about what might have once been a splendid post office during British rule. They saw heavy files tied together with strings, dusty old books and letters bound together in envelopes that had yellowed with time.

It was as if people had abandoned this place in a hurry and had never returned.

'I wonder what happened here,' thought Renu, looking for possible clues.

Aru, in the meantime, was inspecting a wooden door in a far corner, near the backyard. He stomped his foot on it a few times to make sure it was sturdy.

'It's a trap door!' he exclaimed. 'Over here!'
THUMP THUMP!

Aru jostled the wooden door with all his might.

As soon as Manu, Renu and Hari took a step towards him, they heard a shrill screech. It sounded part-human, part-animal and part-something they had never heard before.

They knew it was coming closer. Exactly like the traveller had narrated.

Aru was the first to bolt towards the main door, pushing Hari aside. The three followed him out and sprinted towards their village.

It was raining heavily by the time the friends, soaking and muddy, returned to their orphanage. They climbed the gate and sneaked into their bunk beds quietly, and no one found out they had been missing.

The next morning, Aru tried to avoid meeting his friends. When Hari and Manu confronted him, he finally burst into tears.

'I'm sorry,' he begged them. 'I can't believe I made us all go there in the first place. It's giving me nightmares,' he sobbed.

'It's all right, Aru, we shouldn't have acted like fools ourselves and followed,' said Manu, his voice quivering.

Just then, Renu called out to her brother.

'Hari, come fast! I can't find it,' she cried. 'Our father's watch!'

Hari's face changed.

Their father's watch was the one precious and invaluable

memory of their deceased parents. The siblings had kept it safely with them ever since they could remember.

'I had it yesterday when we went to that cursed bungalow,' she looked at Aru, her eyes flashing angrily. 'In our frenzy, I must have dropped it somewhere along the way. I remember it being in my pocket last at the bungalow,' she said.

'Oh no, you have dropped it at the daak ghar!' Aru exclaimed, as he realized this folly.

'I don't care. We have to go back and find it,' said Renu, determined.

'You have gone mad, Renu. You saw what happened. We could have been killed yesterday by...by...whatever it is that haunts the daak ghar,' said Hari.

'Aru, this is all your fault,' cried Renu. 'You got us into this mess and now you have to get us out. You are coming with us to find the timepiece.'

'No way. I am never going back. Call me whatever you want. I'll never go there,' Aru dug his heels in the ground and crossed his hands over his chest.

'Go where?' the warden of the orphanage overheard them speaking.

'The cursed daak ghar,' said Manu and immediately put his hand on his mouth, realizing what he had said.

'What! You cannot possibly think of it. There have been murders, and I have heard of humans being skinned alive there. Can you imagine?' the warden shook his head.

The children stood open-mouthed, thinking of the bone they had found.

'Ask the postman himself. His forefathers actually worked there when it was functional during the British rule. He knows more about it than anyone else,' the warden said.

Later that day, the four friends set out to meet the village postman, hoping that he would help them.

The postman was a very busy chap. They waited for him all day at the post office until finally, he agreed to see them. They introduced themselves quickly and told him all about their misadventure.

'Stop it!' the postman bellowed, interrupting their story. 'You have no idea about the kind of trouble you are getting into,' he said, grimly. 'That daak ghar is not only cursed and haunted, but also has evil magical powers. Do you remember the traveller mentioning 'letters' over and over again?' he asked the frightened children. 'Do you know what he meant?'

They shook their heads slowly.

'Whoever dares to trespass the boundary of the daak ghar gets a mysterious letter in his name, which means he is the next victim of the blood-sucking ghouls that live there. They know who you are, and they have no mercy.'

All four of them gulped, trying to imagine what could have happened to them if they had stayed longer.

On their way back from the post office, the four friends huddled together.

'I know the dangers of going back there but we have left the one and only symbol of our parents in that wretched house,' said Renu tearfully. 'I have to go back.'

Hari chipped in, 'Sister, I will go with you. I understand

if Aru and Manu do not wish to come along. After all, we are asking them to risk their lives and it is not fair.'

'I'll come,' said Manu. 'We are in this together.'

'All right, I'll come too,' said Aru reluctantly. 'But this time, we will take more torches.'

The rest nodded. They needed to be prepared this time.

Frightened as they were, the four friends were more united than ever now.

They set out in the evening, tough as it was to give the warden a slip. They moved swiftly this time because they knew exactly where the daak ghar was.

Quietly, they approached the clearing, making sure to be as nimble-footed as possible. They didn't want to disturb the spirits. They had simply come to look for the timepiece.

The bungalow was eerily quiet, as if even the spirits were away that night. A stray owl hooted in the distance. The damp walls emitted a foul smell, and they could hear frogs croaking in the dank corners of the house.

The four flashed their torches from side to side, looking for Renu's memento.

Suddenly, Renu caught a glimpse of something that made her eyes grow wide. The large wooden beam that was swinging wildly from the ceiling yesterday, was now fixed in place, back on the ceiling!

The four didn't exchange a word and communicated only through gestures and signs. They split in four directions, beginning to look everywhere for the gold timepiece.

They retraced their steps from the previous night, flashing their torches over books, files, tables and chairs.

A black cat meowed in a corner and Renu followed her to a pile of dusty papers.

Hari looked back to check on his sister, and at that moment, to his utter surprise, she let out a blood-curdling scream—a scream so loud and so frightening that it shook the foundation of the house. The cat shrieked and ran out of their way.

By the time the three boys gathered around her, she was shaken, her face was pale, and her eyes were full of frightened tears.

Her hands trembled, as she held out four envelopes for them to see.

Aru. Hari. Renu. Manu.

Letters addressed to them, found in the dusty old pile in the daak ghar, from a time even before their parents had been born.

Hari grabbed her hand, dropped the letters and ran out of the house, the two others close on their heels. They didn't stop till they were safe in their beds, back in the orphanage.

In the meantime, on the top floor of the daak ghar, a small gas oil lamp burned brightly. The same postman from the village post office and his wife were having a quiet dinner inside.

'They are just kids, you know. I feel bad scaring the heck out of them,' the postman's wife said. 'Moreover, the screeching has made my throat so dry,' she coughed.

'Keep quiet, woman,' snarled the postman. 'Those pesky kids deserved it. Hope they learnt their lesson not to intrude, just like that annoying traveller. I tried to warn them after all. We should have just trapped him there in that pit.'

The woman shook her head, knowing her husband actually enjoyed scaring intruders away. It has been his little game for years.

'As for us, just be happy we have a place to stay, rent-free. It's technically government property, you know. We are occupying it illegally,' he said. 'Oh, look what I found this time—this antique gold timepiece! The ghosts of daak ghar will now have a fancy sense of style too,' he laughed uproariously as his voice echoed through the desolate daak ghar.

3.
The Great Himalayan Explorer

TING TINGTINGTINGTINGTINGTING

The school bell rang loudly in the courtyard, echoing along the narrow lanes of Milam, a tiny village in Pithoragarh.

The lunch bell was always followed by the joyful squeal of children, happy to be relieved from their classes and excited to see what their mothers had packed in their tiffin boxes.

But no one was more relieved than three boys kneeling outside the headmaster's room, their hands holding their ears, elbows jutting outwards.

'Finally!' whispered one of the boys. 'I have never waited for the lunch bell this badly before.'

'I know! This headmaster better let us go. We have been punished for an hour now!' said another.

'Shhhh, quiet! I can hear him. He is coming out,' the third boy warned them.

The headmaster took his time to step out of his room.

The three boys could hear him shuffle a few papers around.

'He is just so unfair!' said the first boy again. 'Just because we took a detour on our way to school and missed the morning class does not mean we deserve this punishment, right?'

'My knees hurt! Such a big punishment for such a small crime,' sighed the second boy. 'That big, mustachioed, boring, old man! Ha! What does he know about adventure?'

'Moreover, we were only exploring our village, discovering a new place that no one knows about. If you ask me, I think we were doing this village a favour!' said the third.

'Do you mean you were on an expedition?' the headmaster's sharp voice startled the boys.

He walked up to face the three boys, who were now perspiring profusely. But instead of giving them a harsh scolding, the headmaster plonked down in front of them, cross-legged.

Hands still clutching their ears and knees grazing the floor, the three boys stared wide-eyed at their headmaster, bewildered.

'Do you know what true exploration means, boys?' he asked. The boys shook their heads.

'Then you haven't heard of the greatest Himalayan explorer we have ever known—Nain Singh Rawat, who by the way, hailed from this very village!' said the headmaster.

'What did he explore? Where did he go?' asked the first boy.

'He was the first man in the world to explore Tibet

on foot, all by himself! During British rule in India, this man was sent to measure the distance and altitude and also map the rivers of the entire country, all by himself,' said the headmaster.

'How did he do it? Did he take a lot of equipment to measure all this?' asked the second boy, imagining a man carrying long measuring tapes and tall foot rulers whilst climbing the rugged mountains of Tibet.

'Oh no, no equipment, son,' said the headmaster. 'He was trained to measure each step in exactly 33 inches and for each step, he would count one bead of his rosary. He was able to cover exactly 1.6 kilometres in 2000 steps! That is how he kept an account of how much distance he covered in a day.'

'Huh! That's absurd. How did he know he was going in the correct direction? What if he kept going around in circles? Didn't he get confused?' asked the third boy, finding the headmaster's story difficult to believe.

'Oh, he was a man of extraordinary intelligence,' said the headmaster. 'He had learnt how to identify all the major stars and different constellations in order to guide him forward in the right direction.'

'But what about during the day when there are no stars?' asked the second boy, astonished.

'He had a small compass attached to his prayer wheel and he also hid mercury inside a few cowrie shells to determine temperature and altitude.'

'But punditji (sir), why did he have a prayer wheel and cowrie shells and rosary beads with him? I thought you

said he was an explorer, not a saint or an ascetic,' asked the third boy.

The headmaster smiled.

'That was the most important part of his mission. He was travelling and exploring Tibet under the disguise of a Buddhist monk! You see, Tibet did not allow citizens of other countries to come and map their territory,' said the headmaster, 'So, he had to do it undercover.'

'So, are you saying he was a spy?' asked the first boy.

'Yes indeed, for the government. He couldn't afford to reveal his true identity, so he made notes about his travels, rolled them up into tiny scrolls and hid them inside the hollow cylinder of his prayer wheel.'

The boys looked at each other, wide-eyed.

'What's more, he had to encounter life-threatening dangers such as fierce Himalayan predators, poisonous snakes, scorpions and even hostile tribes in the hinterland.'

'The incredible Himalayan spy-explorer!' exclaimed the third boy.

'Yes, and because of his bravery and intelligence, we now know that Tsangpo, the great Tibetan river, is the same as the Brahmaputra in India,' said the headmaster.

'Oh! The Brahmaputra—one of the longest and most important rivers in India!' exclaimed one of the boys.

'Yes! Moreover, after his mission to Tibet, he was also part of the Great Trigonometrical Survey of India, an ambitious task to measure the entire Indian subcontinent, as far back in 1802!'

'That's incredible! And to think, he was from our own

village!' the boys exclaimed.

'Oh and one more thing,' said the headmaster, disappearing into the room.

'This is for you boys, to remind you of Nain Singh Rawat and his incredible explorations,' the headmaster said, brandishing a simple, but beautiful Buddhist prayer wheel in his hand.

'Is this the same...?' asked one of the boys in awe.

'Yes, this is indeed the same prayer wheel he used on his travels, undercover,' said the headmaster smiling.

'But how did it get here?' asked another boy.

'Well, I am proud to say that there was a time in his life when the great Nain Singh Rawat served as headmaster of this very school!' the headmaster exclaimed.

The boys gasped and murmured excitedly, 'He was headmaster of our school at one time?'

The headmaster nodded. 'By the way, your punishment is over now; you may leave.'

'I just hope you now realize that big, mustachioed, boring, old headmasters do know a thing or two about adventure!' he laughed, as the boys ran to their classroom clutching Nain Singh Rawat's prayer wheel in their hands, along with a piece of history.

This story is based on the real life story of Indian explorer and surveyor, Nain Singh Rawat (1830-1882), who hailed from Pithoragarh in Uttarakhand.

4.
The Snow Leopard

She was fondly called Ama (grandmother) by everyone in the village. Pleasantly plump, she had eyes that sparkled even as her smile branched out to crow's feet. She loved the company of children, especially because she loved telling stories.

Ama was a beauty for her age, which, by the way, was anyone's guess. She never brought it up and no one dared ask her how old she was.

Every Sunday, children came in big groups to listen to her stories. They sipped warm water and ginger in her little backyard, while she narrated fascinating tales from the Himalayas.

On one such Sunday, she asked the children gathered in her house, 'Has anyone ever seen a snow leopard?'

The children looked at each other and shook their heads. They had heard about the majestic snow leopards that lived high up in the snowy mountain peaks, but no one had ever seen one.

Perhaps there were very few left now, and perhaps no one dared to venture that high up in the mountains where it was difficult to breathe.

Some children even believed that they never actually existed.

'Oh, but they did,' said Ama, her eyes twinkling.

'They are beautiful, magnificent beasts with white and ash-grey coats and black twirls for spots. They are a bit smaller than the leopards in our forests but much more intelligent.'

The children squealed and urged her to tell them a story about these mysterious creatures.

She began.

'Almost a hundred years ago, on the snowy mountain tops of the Nanda Devi mountain, lived a small nomadic tribe. They were the last survivors of an ancient tribe that had lived and travelled across the harsh mountain terrain, looking for food and shelter.

The tribe had created a small commune in a remote nook of the mountain, with just a few pine trees as cover against the chilly winds. Most of the ground was covered with a thick layer of snow throughout the year.

In the tribe, lived a little girl, with her father, the chief, her mother and their yak, Oku. Every day, she would take Oku to graze in a small meadow nearby and help her mother fetch fresh snow for water.

One winter evening, as the little girl was returning home with Oku, she suddenly realized that the sun had almost set. The girl did her best to rush the yak, but he seemed to be in no mood to hurry up. With each tug of the rope tied around his neck, he dug his feet even deeper into the snow, refusing to buck up.

She knew they were in trouble because the sky was changing colour from peach to purple and soon it would turn dark blue, which was curfew time for the tribe. According to the tribe's rules, everyone had to be back in the commune as soon as the sky turned a particular shade of blue—for it meant it was officially dusk, the hour of predators.

The hooves of the yak and the footsteps of the little girl had made deep shapes in the snow, but the shadowy blue light made it difficult for the girl to retrace her steps back home. As she squinted to focus her vision on her steps, suddenly, she stopped in her tracks.

There was a third set of impressions alongside hers and Oku's.

These were giant marks, set deep in the snow. Confused, she took a look around her, wondering if the dark shadows were playing tricks on her mind. There was no one else around.

The marks made a sharp turn just ahead and vanished before a patch of jagged rocks jutting out of the snow.

Oku sensed something was amiss and dug his heels deeper in the snow. He bellowed, refusing to move ahead.

Just then, the two heard a deep, throaty growl coming from inside a crack in the rocks.

The little girl let go of Oku's rope and approached the rocks slowly and cautiously.

She was not prepared for what she saw.

A stunning snow leopard, ash grey in colour with black markings that looked like pencil shavings across its body, lay there growling. One of its paws was stuck between two large boulders.

The girl felt her heart practically stop beating.

She let out a gasp so soft that it could have been a whisper, but the leopard turned his head sharply and looked straight at her.

Their eyes met for a split second and the leopard growled again, only louder this time.

It was both the most beautiful and the most terrifying creature she had ever seen. Its eyes were a deep shade of green that glowed in the dim light, and its thick fur had flakes of snow on it. Its tail, long and heavy, was moving restlessly—the creature itself was whining in pain.

They were just eight steps apart. He could pounce on her in one clean leap and she and poor Oku would promptly turn into his dinner.

Another growl snapped her out of her shock. She turned to leave but a nagging thought stopped her in her tracks.

'What if his paw is stuck here for days? He will die of hunger and pain,' she thought.

Despite her fear, she stepped slowly and cautiously towards the leopard.

When she was just two steps away, she stretched her body sideways to reach one of the boulders between which his paw was trapped. She couldn't push it away; it was too heavy.

The leopard's green eyes were transfixed on her.

'He will not survive, if someone doesn't help him. But if I help him, he might kill me instead,' she thought, shuddering.

The boulder she was trying to move still didn't budge.

Quickly, she backed down and ran to Oku. She took one end of the long rope that was tied around him, looped it around the boulder and signalled for the yak to walk in the opposite direction.

Terrified by the predator's growls, the yak was more than keen to rush home, so he pulled with all his might, until the rock gave way and the leopard's paw came free.

The yak sprinted for his life, with the rope flying behind him as the leopard limped out of the crevice slowly.

The girl leaped out of there as soon as she could, cutting and bruising her legs on the jagged rocks as she hurried. She made a final leap and landed on her feet on the soft snow, sprinting home after Oku. She was too terrified to look over her shoulders and see if the leopard was following them.

She kept running with all the energy she could muster until she reached home.

The next morning, she knew she had it coming. Her father, the tribe chief, was furious.

'I never thought you could be so irresponsible! How could you stay out this late? If the yak didn't obey you, you could have returned home, and somebody could have gone to fetch him.'

She had never seen Father so angry before. For a minute, she regretted telling everyone what had happened.

'What if the leopard had attacked you? What were you even thinking?' exclaimed Mother, tears welling up in her eyes.

The little girl's heart sank. She didn't expect everyone to be so upset.

'Mother, I am sorry. I just wanted to help,' she said, in a small voice.

'Help? You put yourself in such grave danger to help whom? A predator? Do you realize you have put all our lives in danger too?' Father interjected.

'The safety of the entire tribe is at stake now. The leopard must have followed you and now knows we live here—it might come to hunt tomorrow. We have to leave this place right away. It is too risky for us and for our animals,' he said, grimly.

The decision had been made. After all, he couldn't risk the lives of the tribe due to his daughter's mistake.

The next morning, the little girl packed up her belongings and set out with the rest of the tribe on their journey to find a new home in the mountains.

Filled with guilt and remorse for having displaced the entire tribe, she trudged along slowly. With their tents and spears, the tribe marched along the snowy ridge of the mountain in a single line.

It was cold and windy and the snow was starting to melt in the morning sun, making the path slippery.

As the tribe trekked uphill, suddenly, there was a loud scream and some commotion towards the back of the line.

One of their tribesmen had slipped and fallen down the ridge! He had tumbled down the snowy slope at breakneck speed, disappearing out of sight in no time.

Horrified, the tribe followed the man down the steep slope, hoping he had survived the fall. They stepped cautiously downhill, but the melting snow made them slip and slide down the mountain.

The girl followed the tribe in the slide downhill, clutching her mother's hand. One after another, they landed in a dark pit. They called out his name but couldn't see or hear a thing.

Then they heard something that made a chill run down their spines. They knew what it was—the growls of snow leopards, definitely more than one.

One of the tribesmen managed to light a torch stick.

Much to their horror, the tribe realized they were all standing in a large leopard's lair and staring straight into six pairs of fierce green eyes.

The men and women immediately grabbed their bows and arrows while the beasts growled and bared their teeth, threatening to attack their intruders.

Just then with a big thump, the biggest and mightiest of the leopards appeared out of the darkness. With an air of authority, he stepped out in front of the other leopards. The tribesmen knew this was the leader.

Watching from a distance with her mother, the little girl instantly realized this was the leopard she had encountered. There was something remarkable about him. She wondered if it was the deep green eyes that she had seen so closely just the previous day.

Without warning, she darted out, past all the other men and women and managed to stand right next to her father. She pulled her shoulders back and tilted her chin upwards, looking straight into the magnificent creature's eyes.

The tribe gasped as they saw the girl confront the beast.

Before they could understand what was happening, the tribe saw the snow leopard turn towards his pack and retreat further into the lair, disappearing into the darkness. All the other leopards followed suit.

The tribesmen picked up the man who had slipped and fallen into the lair, and started to climb out of the ditch, one after the other.'

• ◆

'What about the girl, Ama? Did the tribe realize that it was the same leopard she had helped the previous day?' asked one of the children who were listening to the story.

'Yes, they did. And the tribe was full of praise for the girl for her act of kindness which saved them all,' said Ama. 'Her father was stunned but proud of his daughter.'

'That was lovely, Ama,' exclaimed another child. 'But how do you know if the story is true?'

'Because, my dear child,' said Ama, smiling, as she sipped her warm ginger tea. 'I was that little girl.'

The children gasped.

'And yes, I am just a little over a hundred,' she said with a wink. 'Thank you for not asking.'

With that, she bid the children goodbye, promising them another evening of stories the next Sunday.

5.
Mischievous Teeth

Deep in a valley, there stood a creaking wooden house, bursting with twenty mischievous brothers and sisters. Their parents lived and worked in the city, so this naughty group of unruly children was under the care of their grandfather, whom they fondly called 'Bubu'.

Now Bubu loved the children very much, but he was constantly besieged by villagers complaining about his mischievous grandchildren.

The twenty siblings—Atsu, Batsu, Catsu, Datsu, Etsu, Fatsu, Gatsu, Hatsu, Jatsu, Katsu, Latsu, Matsu, Natsu, Patsu, Ratsu, Satsu, Tatsu, Vatsu, Yatsu and Zatsu would create utter chaos in the neighbourhood.

Some of them would knock on their neighbours' doors and run away when someone answered it, others would steal the school bell and ring it every 5 minutes, sending the village school into a tizzy. On some days, the children would steal fruits from the village orchards and on others, they would give wrong directions to visitors, only to have them roaming the village in circles.

There were new complaints every day and Bubu was fed up. One day, he decided to teach the kids a lesson.

'Pair up in twos,' he ordered them, first thing in the morning.

'From now on, you will play with only one partner each. I have cast a spell on all of you so that if you make any mischief, the pair will lose its teeth—two at a time. Be warned!'

The children looked at each other and shrugged. They guessed Bubu was just trying to scare them into behaving well.

Nevertheless, they paired up in twos and went to play.

Atsu and Batsu went over to the nearby lake and saw three villagers bathing in the water. Their clothes lay on the grass nearby, along with their wallets.

The brother and sister sneaked up behind a bush and stole all their belongings. They hid everything behind a few bushes far away and ran home. They laughed on their way home, thinking about what would happen when the villagers realized their clothes were missing.

'They won't even have money to buy new clothes. We hid their wallets too!' Batsu said, sending her brother into a fit of laughter.

But suddenly, in the midst of his open-mouthed laugh, Atsu let out a loud yelp.

'ACKKKK! My tooth,' he cried.

'Why does it seem like it's coming loose?' he asked aloud, petrified. 'Look, it is moving,' he gasped.

'Mine too!' exclaimed Batsu, while yanking her lower front tooth.

By the time they reached home, Atsu and Batsu had lost two front teeth each.

In the meantime, Catsu and Datsu were up to their own mischief.

They went up to the neighbourhood tea stall and replaced all the sugar with salt. When the vendor returned to make some tea for his customers, Catsu and Datsu hung around to see what would happen.

One customer spat out the tea in his mouth. Another stuck out his tongue and hopped about on his feet, leaving the poor vendor bewildered.

'Salty tea couldn't have tasted nice,' laughed Catsu.

'OUCH!' yelled Datsu. 'My tooth, Catsu! OUCH!'

'Mine too!' cried Catsu. 'Look! It's coming off.'

In another part of the village, Etsu and Fatsu lost their teeth too—the ones on the sides of their lower front teeth. They had just strategically placed banana peels on the pavement to watch someone slip and fall.

Gatsu and Hatsu were rolling down the slippery hillside on a wooden plank, destroying their neighbour's well-kept garden, while Jatsu and Katsu had made garlands out of their slippers for the same neighbour's goats.

One by one, all of the children lost two of their teeth—some canines, some incisors, some molars and some premolars.

They all rushed back home crying.

'Ugh, it looks ugly!' said sisters Latsu and Matsu together, examining the gaps in their mouths.

Natsu and Patsu came running back from the community well, where they had thrown pots of ink to make the water turn blue.

'Bubu was right! The spell is real!' said Ratsu and Satsu, now frightened.

'Maybe we should stop now, before it is too late,' said Tatsu. Along with Vatsu, he had just locked someone inside a common bathroom.

'Let's go plead with Bubu to break this spell,' said Yatsu, and Zatsu nodded, still holding his tooth in his hand.

Back at the house, Bubu was dealing with a large crowd of complaining villagers.

There were the three men from the lake who were trying to cover themselves with large banana leaves after finding their clothes had gone missing, a few women whose mouths had blue ink all over them and the angry tea vendor who had served his customers some very questionable tea.

The kids didn't find things so funny this time. And every time they wanted to laugh, they remembered their broken teeth.

After making the children apologize to the villagers, Bubu gathered them in the backyard together.

'Open your mouths,' he commanded. The children obeyed. He couldn't help but chuckle.

'The spell can only be broken with good behaviour,' he said. 'If you stop making mischief, your teeth will slowly grow back. If you continue your pranks, however, you'll keep losing your teeth in twos,' he said.

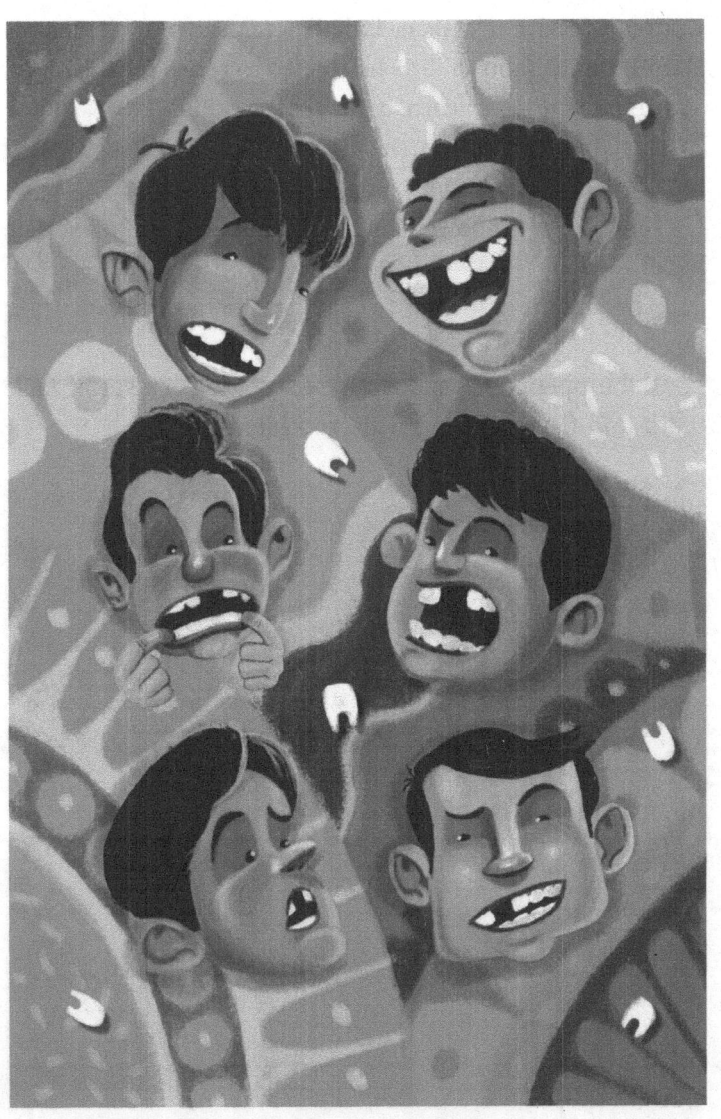

'We are sorry, Bubu. We will be good from now on. We want our teeth back, please!' all the children cried in unison.

'All right,' Bubu said, as he turned to retire for the night. 'It seems you have learnt your lesson, kids.'

Just before turning the lights off, he looked back at his crew one last time.

'But do you know who has been the naughtiest one here?'

The children looked at each other and shook their heads.

Bubu opened his mouth wide, took off his set of false teeth and flashed a big, wide toothless grin.

6.
The Villain

One afternoon, Kamli was reading her book at home, when the door to their little house burst open.

Her sister, little Kisna was back from school. But instead of greeting Kamli, she ran past her into the bathroom and latched the door shut with a loud thud.

Much to her surprise, Kamli heard her little sister sobbing uncontrollably behind the bathroom door.

'Open the door, Kisna. Please! What's wrong? Why are you crying?' asked Kamli, worried.

'No, it's nothing, just go away,' Kisna mumbled between her sobs.

'Kisna, please come out and talk to me,' ordered Kamli firmly.

She hated to see her little sister this upset. As far as Kamli knew, her sister was a mischievous, fun-loving girl who always had a smile on her face.

'Who or what could have hurt her so badly?' wondered Kamli.

After a while, Kisna unlocked the bathroom door herself and walked out, head hung low and shoulders slumped.

'I don't want to talk about anything. Just forget it,' said Kisna before Kamli had a chance to say anything. Kisna quietly stepped out into their backyard to play with her best friend, Kallu the dog.

Kamli was always slightly jealous that her little sister preferred the company of Kallu instead of her.

'But atleast she has stopped crying,' Kamli thought.

The next morning, while getting ready for school, Kamli saw her little sister do something strange. Kisna was looking at her reflection in the mirror and was scrubbing her face with soap so harshly that Kamli thought her skin might peel off.

She scrubbed and scrubbed as if she were trying to scrape her skin off.

Kamli was shocked, but she didn't confront her sister. Instead, she decided to do a little spying to find out what was going on. The same day at school, Kamli sneaked into her little sister's classroom at lunchtime. She hid under a desk to observe.

A big group of students and teachers had gathered in a corner of the classroom and were discussing something animatedly. The rest of the class was scattered and Kisna was nowhere to be seen.

Kamli was puzzled. Where was her sister? Just as she was about to give up and leave, she noticed a group of students practising a play for the school's upcoming annual day.

'Sita, O Sita! Where are you, my beloved?' said a boy loudly.

'Help! Help! I am being kidnapped by the cruel Ravan! Help!' cried a girl dramatically.

'They are practising the Ram Leela,' Kamli realized. 'But where's my little Kisna? Since she is brilliant at dance and dramatics, she must have a good role in this play.'

Kamli looked around the room once again, and finally spotted her sister sitting slumped in the far corner of the class, her head resting on the desk, turned away from everyone.

Kamli's heart sank. She knew something was gravely wrong with her sister. Maybe this is why she came home crying yesterday.

That afternoon when Kisna returned from school, Kamli was waiting for her.

'I came to your classroom today, Kisna. I saw how everyone is performing the Ram Leela for the school's function. I didn't see you participate. Why?'

'Oh I didn't want to be a part of it,' said Kisna, looking down at her shoes.

'I know how much you like this story because you enacted an entire scene from this story yourself as three different characters during our picnic last year,' Kamli challenged her.

'Fine,' said Kisna, slumping on the stool next to Kamli. 'They hated me,' she said, her voice trembling. 'I tried out for the role of Sita yesterday and the entire class laughed at me.'

'What? Why did they laugh?' Kamli asked, puzzled since she knew what a good actor Kisna was.

Kisna's eyes welled up with tears as she told Kamli what had happened. 'Some of my classmates said Sita is meant to be pretty and dainty, while I am dark-skinned and big,' said Kisna in a small voice.

'They were all laughing at me because I tried to get the role of the beautiful lady,' Kisna was sobbing now, 'when, clearly, I'm not suited for it. Oh, why am I like this?' Kisna asked between sobs.

Kamli was shocked to hear this. She grabbed Kisna's hand and dragged the sobbing girl to the backyard, where Kallu the dog came to greet them enthusiastically. He sensed Kisna was distressed so he started licking her feet, trying to calm her down.

'Look at Kallu,' said Kamli. 'Look at how happy he is to see you and look at how he's trying to console you.'

Kisna stroked the dog's head, trying to reassure him despite herself.

'To him, you are the kindest, nicest soul in the world and he loves you for being you, exactly the way you are. That means the colour of your skin, your height, your weight—everything that makes you unique.'

'But why am I not pretty like the girl who got Sita's part? I wanted that role! I even memorized all her lines!' A fresh stream of warm tears started to roll down her cheeks again.

'Kisna, listen to me,' said Kamli.

'Take a look at Kallu again. His shaggy mane, that black

patch on his nose and think of his goofy antics. Would you rather he be a perfectly groomed, spotless, manicured, perfectly behaved dog instead?'

'No! I love him exactly the way he is,' said Kisna, wiping her tears. 'Those are the things about him that I love the most!'

'That's what I'm talking about!' exclaimed Kamli.

'Everything about you makes you unique, special and loveable. Your skin is dark because it protects you against the sun, so you can play outside as much as you want. Your skin will stay beautiful even when you are an old lady. It's Mother Nature's gift to you, little one,' Kamli explained. 'It makes you unique and special and beautiful!'

'And you are big, robust and strong, so that no one can mess with you; in fact, you'll be able to beat anyone at a wrestling match, hands down!'

Kisna giggled despite herself because she knew it was true.

'I saw you trying to scrub your face with soap this morning. What were you trying to do? Change your appearance? Imagine if one day you actually start looking different, poor Kallu would not recognize you and would go looking for his friend—the Kisna he knows and loves, exactly the way she is, because of the way she is,' Kamli said, smiling.

Kisna kissed the dog on his head and hugged her sister.

'You are right,' she said. 'I am what I am, and one thing I know is that I am a good actor. And I will be part of my school play, one way or the other.'

Kamli was thrilled to see her sister's change in attitude.

'I know what to do now,' Kisna said with a small giggle and whispered something in Kamli's ears.

The next day, as the class was about to begin practising for the play, they had a surprise visitor.

Kisna entered the room with a loud thud, took a deep breath and bellowed, speaking from her belly.

'Demon king and beast of beasts,

Fierce and fearless, given to feasts.

My powers and skills brought me fame,

Bow down, people, RAVAN is my name.'

The room was stunned into silence until one of the students finally spoke, 'Ravan is a man. You can't play his role!'

'Yes!' another classmate chimed in. 'He is a fierce demon king and you are a girl,' she said.

'Oh but boys have been playing girls' roles on stage for centuries. After all, as actors it is our job to simply act,' said Kisna, smiling.

They couldn't argue with that.

'Besides, my skin is dark, mysterious and fierce. And didn't you all say yourselves that I am robust and well-built? Why, these qualities are perfect for the role of the mighty Ravan, right?'

The classmates blinked, not knowing what to say.

'Oh and I can do a demon laugh too,' she said.

'MWAHAHAHAHAHAHA,' sending the room into amused laughter.

The teacher nodded. 'Very well, Kisna. You are our

Ravan.' She was secretly relieved because no one else had volunteered to play the role of the villain.

As the days passed and they practised for the school play, Kisna made up her own dialogues and helped the others with theirs. They cut out cardboard pieces together to make trees and huts and animals. The performance was going to be the biggest day of their little lives, after all.

However, when the big day finally arrived, things didn't go quite as planned.

The entire school, from class one to class ten, all the teachers, including the school headmaster were sitting in the audience.

The actors were nervous as the curtains opened and the play began.

Much to their dismay, the dhoti of the boy who was playing Ram, came loose and fell off, Hanuman forgot his dialogues and to top it off, the cardboard trees toppled offstage.

Everything that could possibly go wrong, actually did.

There was chaos on stage and laughter from the audience until a loud, booming voice took over the auditorium.

'MWAHAHAHAHAHAHA!' Ravan bellowed, stunning the crowd into silence. The audience sat up in rapt attention, in awe of the fierce and mighty demon king. They watched in silence as Ravan dragged Sita away.

The crowd's attentiveness gave the other actors the confidence to do their best.

After the hero defeated the villain in the final battle

and the mighty army of make-believe monkeys retreated, the curtains were drawn, and all the actors took a bow.

The audience cheered and clapped the loudest for Ravan. Kisna, under her disguise, had eyes only for her sister, and tried to locate her amongst the sea of smiling faces.

Before she knew it, Kisna realized she was being carried on her classmates' shoulders as they went backstage. 'Ravan! Ravan! Ravan saved the day!' they chanted, even as Kisna tried to balance her ten cardboard heads.

Suddenly, she saw Kamli waiting backstage with open arms, a huge basket by her side.

'You missed the applause!' said Kisna, pouting. 'Where were you?'

'I didn't need to be there to know that the loudest cheers were for the fiercest villain,' said Kamli with a wink, giving her sister a tight hug.

'By the way, look who came to congratulate you,' she said, as Kallu leaped out of the big basket to give his fierce and mighty Kisna the biggest cuddle he could.

'Thank you Kallu. Thank you for being you.' she whispered in his ear. 'And for showing me, how to be me.'

7.
The Long-Lost Friends

It was almost summer, and I couldn't wait to visit my uncle's village again—the last and most remote village, just before the Pindari glacier.

I wondered if my old friends, Rana and Gobind and the twins, Bisnu and Kanta still remembered me. It had been two years since my last visit.

'They have probably forgotten all about me and our little secret,' I thought. We used to write letters to each other every month until they abruptly stopped replying to me last year.

'Never mind,' I consoled myself. I was just glad that I would see them again soon. 'What a surprise it will be!' I thought as I stuck my head out of the bus window, feeling the cool, crisp air tickle my face.

The bus came to a squealing, creaking stop on the second-last station of its route. From there, it was a long walk on a winding road uphill, flanked by rows of flowering shrubs. I had looked forward to picking the bright yellow hisalu berries for a snack, but as soon as I stepped off the bus, I knew something was wrong.

'What happened here?' I whispered, as I surveyed the pathway. Much to my dismay, the once beautiful pathway was covered in gravel and rocks—there were no green shrubs in sight, much less my favourite yellow berries.

When I reached the village, I could tell something was different. How could it have changed so much in just two years? 'Maybe I am just very hungry and don't remember right,' I thought, trying to shrug off the hollow feeling in my stomach.

By the time I reached my uncle's familiar bright blue wooden house, it had become dark and very, very quiet. All the birds had suddenly vanished from the pink sky.

'Welcome back, son!' Uncle swung the door open and welcomed me with a tight hug.

As I lay on the jute charpoy (a light bedstead) on the terrace after dinner, I remembered the last time I had stared up at a glittering night sky, just like this one.

That night all those years ago, the gas lantern on the table had hissed loudly and a dozen fireflies had been buzzing furiously overhead. But the five of us, Rana, Gobind, Bisnu, Kanta and I had been too busy to be distracted by the noise. We were trying to draw a map on a paper with a piece of charcoal.

I smiled, remembering how it took us hours to draw, redraw and correct it before we had finally agreed upon the drawing. Bisnu had folded the paper into a little boat and buried it deep under a banyan tree, not far from my uncle's house.

'I wonder if it's still there,' I thought, drifting off to sleep under the night sky.

The next morning, I got dressed to go find the four of them, hoping they would be as excited to see me as I was at the prospect of seeing them.

'Heading out, son? Don't venture too far and whatever you do, do not go upstream!' Uncle called after me, but I was already on my way out.

As I walked further uphill, closer to the purple-flower field we used to play in, I saw the houses we would pass by. The brick and stone shanties that had once been warm and noisy were now dark and empty, strangely even in the morning sun.

It was so silent that I could hear a faint cawing in the distance, but it wasn't the birdsong of a mountain cuckoo. It sounded more like a bird of prey to me. There was not a single human in sight.

I shrugged and walked further uphill, past the deserted field to our beloved stream, hoping to find my friends there.

The stream was swollen and thick, rushing furiously down the boulders. I stopped for a drink of its icy cool water and continued to walk upstream.

'I ought to find them here,' I thought. I was sure their house had been just around the corner, but I couldn't see it now. There was no one to ask. Even the trees seemed to have gone missing.

'What on Earth has happened to this place?' I looked around stunned.

Just then, a loud thumping sound from behind me made me whip my head around. The sharp, afternoon sun cast shadows on the figure before me, so I couldn't tell if it was a mountain bear or a boy. As I squinted to adjust to the bright sun, my eyes widened, and I squealed, 'Bisnu!'

I ran towards him and lunged forward to hug him, but Bisnu stepped back. He wasn't smiling. He was wearing a pale blue shirt, which was incidentally what he had been wearing the last time I saw him. And as usual, it had one button missing.

I stepped back too, disappointed that my old friend didn't seem happy to see me.

'Are you all right, Bisnu?' I asked, urging him to look at me. He was trying to avoid looking directly at my face.

'I am all right now,' he said, slowly. 'But I wasn't, for a long time.'

'I wrote to you so many times in the last year, Bisnu! Why didn't you reply?' I asked.

'I...I couldn't reply,' he spoke very slowly.

'What is wrong? Tell me! And where's everyone else?' I was getting impatient. What was wrong with this boy?

Bisnu turned his back towards me, and I followed his gaze. From the shadows, another small figure stepped out into the clearing. I was surprised to see it was his twin sister, Kanta.

She stepped into the light, head bowed, and eyes lowered.

'So, you are back,' she said, quietly.

'Well, yes but will someone please tell me what's going on?' I asked, starting to get annoyed.

She was unsure if she should say anything, I could tell. Her anklets made a jingling sound as she paced back and forth. She still wore a string of champa flowers in her hair and those green bangles I remember her wearing the last time I saw her. She looked exactly the same too.

'There was a massive flood last year, here in our village,' she said in a small, quiet voice. It washed away everything—our homes, our trees and even our people,' she spoke, looking at her feet.

'What! Dear God! Do we know anyone who was affected? What about Rana and Gobind? Where are they? How are they?'

The twins looked at each other for a long time before answering, 'They are gone too.'

Shocked and heartbroken, I walked slowly towards the stream and sat down beside its gurgling waters.

A lone tree gave us shade as we sat side by side, our feet dangling in the ice cool water.

We sat quietly for a long time before I broke the silence. 'Do you remember what we found the last time we were here? Do you remember that night under the light of the gas lamp? We only had pieces of charcoal for the drawing.'

'Yes, of course,' said Bisnu, with a small smile. 'The map to the forgotten river—the one we discovered ourselves.'

'We were so excited to have explored the forest on our own and find the enchanted river,' Kanta remembered too. 'The water was so clear, we could see through till the riverbed, with all its orange and yellow fishes swimming by.'

I sprang to my feet. 'Come, let's find it—our map,' I cried, suddenly excited. 'We can dig it out from under the banyan tree where we buried it! Tomorrow, we can follow the directions on the map and find that river again.'

The twins shrugged and followed me towards the banyan tree, near my uncle's house.

We hadn't ventured very far when we heard something directly behind us—the unmistakable low growl of a wild mountain bear.

I knew outrunning it would be impossible and tried to think as quickly as possible.

I caught a glimpse of the brother-sister duo from the corner of my eyes. They were calm and still, almost statue-like, looking straight ahead at the bear who was now standing in front of us.

A split-second later, much to my utter amazement, the bear backed down meekly, retracing its steps!

'What?' I asked the twins, aghast. 'How did you manage to scare the bear away?'

Bisnu shrugged. 'We didn't do anything, it got frightened on its own, I guess.'

Along the way to the banyan tree, we chatted about what I had been up to at school in Nainital. The twins were eager to know about everything. I felt sad, thinking how unfair it was that my friends had not had a normal life after the disaster.

I felt compelled to help them—they had no family left. 'Perhaps my uncle could help by sending them to school,' I thought.

I was relieved to see the banyan tree still standing there, tall and proud—its long, strong roots hanging so low that they almost brushed the ground under them.

I grabbed a long, sharp stone and started digging in the area that, I suspected, had the map underneath. No luck. I tried another spot, but again, I did not find anything. After six more attempts, I looked up to find the twins swinging merrily from the dangling roots of the tree.

'Do you mind giving me a hand?' I asked, getting irritated that they hadn't even offered to help.

They simply giggled and continued to swing.

A passer-by looked at me strangely, having heard me. He looked like he was about to approach us but backed away from us slowly, as if he was afraid for his life.

'People in this village are strange, indeed,' I murmured to myself, as I continued digging.

'Found it, look!' Kanta came running from the other side of the tree.

She laid the map down for us to see.

The charcoal was smeared, and the thick paper was soggy and tattered.

'I'll keep that,' I said, quickly folding the paper back and putting it in my pocket. I wanted to make sure I dried it properly, so we can retrace our steps to the forgotten river. I didn't trust the twins to keep it safely.

'I want to ask you two, would you please come with

me to my uncle's house?' I asked, hoping I could help them in some way.

'It's a little late for that, isn't it?' said Bisnu drily, as Kanta shook her head.

'We can't go with you, we only came to say goodbye, and we are so glad we did,' said Kanta, smiling.

'No, look. That's my uncle's house right there,' I said, turning around to point in the direction of the house.

I turned back to say he would be happy to host us for lunch, but the twins were gone. They just left abruptly, almost vanishing into thin air.

'How silly of them not to accept my help,' I thought. 'And how rude to vanish like that without saying goodbye. I'll give them a piece of my mind tomorrow,' I thought.

I walked to the house annoyed, but excited to have the map back. I wanted to find the forgotten river and take a dip in its magical waters, just like our little gang did two years ago.

Just then, my uncle burst through the door, panting.

'Son! You're all right! Thank heavens!' he said, touching my shoulder to make sure I was fine.

'Yes, of course, I'm all right. What's the matter?' I asked, a bit alarmed.

'My neighbour told me he saw you below the banyan tree—the haunted banyan tree nearby. It looked like you were speaking to someone while digging the ground but there was no one there.'

'What? No, uncle, I was there with my friends, Bisnu and Kanta, and we were just looking for a map we had hidden under the tree.'

I dug my fist into my pocket to find the folded boat map to show him but to my shock, all I found in my palm was a champa flower and a pale blue button instead.

Uncle's face grew pale.

'Bisnu and Kanta?' He gulped. 'Son, Bisnu and Kanta died in the flood last year.'

8.
The Biggest Gift

A small family of farmers lived in Satoli, a small town in Kumaon, known for its fruit orchards. Mother, Father and little Suja lived in a cosy house on one such orchard, where they grew apricots.

Suja watched her parents pick fruit and sell it at the market every week during harvest season. She observed how every morning, her mother would pack a lunchbox for Father with a simple meal and a special treat—his favourite sweet, Bal mithai. To return Mother's loving gesture, Father would pick a bunch of her favourite rhododendron flowers on his way back home.

They were simple and hardworking folk who didn't have time for much other than work and enjoying a good family meal together.

But one day, everything changed for them.

It was the peak of harvest season when Father burst into the house in excitement. 'You won't believe what happened today!' he exclaimed.

'A bus from Binsar came to visit our market. It was full of traders who were looking for the best fruits to sell in the big city. One trader came up to my stall, took a bite out of one of our apricots, and went berserk! He said he had never tasted such delicious apricots before.'

Suja and Mother were delighted. Their hard work had paid off.

'Can you believe he offered to buy our entire stock of apricots? We have sold out this week!' he exclaimed.

'This is great news! Let's celebrate,' Mother said happily.

'But before that, let me show you what I bought for you,' he said, as he pulled out a small box from his pocket.

Mother's eyes grew wide as she opened the box. It was a nath! A beautiful nose ring made of pure gold.

Mother was so happy and astonished that she was speechless for a while.

In Kumaon, the nath has always been considered a symbol of a husband's love for his wife. People believed that the bigger the nath, the more prosperous and affectionate the husband is.

The family celebrated with halwa and kheer that night, something they always lovingly shared on happy occasions. Mother wore the gold nath and looked radiant, not just because of the beautiful piece of jewellery, but because of the joy that reflected on her face.

A week went by and business started to pick up even more. The trader who had bought all their wares came back to buy more apricots from Suja's father.

The Biggest Gift

This time, Father was overjoyed, and he called his family out into the courtyard. 'Suja, Nammu! Come out!'

'What's the matter?' cried Mother.

'Our fortunes have changed, my love. The trader asked me if I would like to sell him our fruit every week from now on,' he said happily.

Mother and Suja were both thrilled.

'We are going to be rich!' he said as little Suja squeezed in to share a family hug.

'Here's something else I bought for you,' he said to Mother, as he pulled out a bigger box from his bag.

Mother couldn't contain her excitement. 'Another gift?' she shrieked in excitement.

'A bigger gift,' said Father.

'Oh Lord!' she gasped as she opened the box. 'This nath is much bigger than the previous one.'

'I know,' said Father. 'Last time I could only afford the small one, but I know how much you liked it so I decided to get a bigger one for you this time.'

Mother's eyes welled up with tears, 'This is the happiest day of my life.'

They forgot all about the kheer and halwa that night, excited about their changing fortune. They chatted the night away, deciding what to do with the extra income.

Six months passed by and their farm's fruit brought them even more money. Their apricot business was booming.

Suja saw that Mother had stopped packing lunchboxes for Father.

'Oh, he will buy something delicious from the market for lunch,' Suja overheard her speaking to the neighbour. 'I don't need to make his lunch anymore.'

With that, another tradition ended—the one where Father brought Mother her favourite flowers on his way back from the market.

Mother hardly seemed to notice though. She was busy planning their next financial move. This time, she asked Father for a bigger nath herself.

'The one with rubies and a string of little pearls in it,' she said, with a twinkle in her eyes.

'Do you really need another one?' asked Father.

'No dear, I don't need one. I want one. After all, we can afford it. I don't see what the problem is,' she said, angry that he had questioned her.

'But just because we can afford it, does not mean we must have it,' Father shrugged.

After a long argument, Father finally gave in.

A new nath came home that day. More opulent than any of the ones before, it was decorated with rubies and a string of pretty, dangling pearls. Suja gasped when she saw it, as it was possibly one of the most beautifully crafted naths in all of Kumaon.

'It covers most of mother's dainty face,' thought Suja. 'How will she eat properly?' she wondered.

But mother wore the nath everywhere, every day.

'Is it not hurting you?' asked Father out of concern.

'Forget that. You should have seen the look on our neighbour's face! She was so jealous, she just kept staring,' said mother, chuckling.

'That is not why I bought you the nath,' Father said, disappointed.

'It does not matter anyhow,' said Mother as Suja saw her father's face fall. He was deeply hurt by her comments.

The final blow came a month later, when Mother asked for yet another gift—an even bigger nath.

Father was furious this time.

'I don't care if we can afford it; I refuse to buy it. It does not make any sense. You have gone mad with greed!' Father lost his temper.

'I have worked just as hard as you have to enjoy this wealth today. I deserve to buy whatever I want, whenever I want!' Mother was equally angry.

Suja heard them fight bitterly from outside the room. Nervous and scared, she hoped the fight would end soon and they could all sit down for their family dinner.

But she sat alone for dinner that night. Mother served her something she had made quickly and retreated for the night. Father sat outside on the porch alone.

The house had never been this quiet and lonely before.

The next evening, as Suja returned from the community school, she saw a gathering of villagers outside her house.

When she ran inside to find her parents, she was shocked.

Mother was lying on the bed, her nose wrapped up in a large white bandage and the village doctor was packing his briefcase and preparing to leave. Father was sitting beside her, shaking his head in dismay.

One by one, the villagers began to leave and Suja got a chance to speak to Mother. 'Ija (mother), what happened? What's wrong with your nose?' she asked, worried.

Mother and Father looked at each other and much to her surprise, burst out laughing.

'My nose fell off under the weight of my stupidity,' said Mother.

Suja nearly screamed, 'What?'

'The heavy nose ring tore the soft skin on her nose and it fell off due to the weight of the rubies and pearls in it,' Father explained.

'Ah but it was partly my fault too,' he added. 'I thought I could show my love and appreciation with the size of the nath. Little did I know it would cost me her lovely nose.'

That night, the family celebrated at home. The grand nose ring was put away in its box, while the house was filled with the aroma of freshly picked rhododendrons, halwa and kheer once again.

9.
Chipko!

'They are coming!'

Little Laali was hurtling down the mountainside, shouting at the top of her voice while slipping and sliding on the loose mud.

'They are coming!' she screamed again, this time within the earshot of a group of women sitting together in a small courtyard.

It was mid-morning, and the women were engrossed in their daily chores—some were knitting, and stitching, while others were gathering wool from their sheep.

Breathless and bruised, Laali tried her best to convey what she had just seen to this group of women.

They gathered around little Laali, alarmed by her screams.

'I just saw them—they are coming in big trucks,' said Laali, huffing and puffing from the run. 'From what I could see, there were at least 50 men and some of them had big, big axes.'

Gaura Devi, one of the oldest in the group, hurried over to Laali.

'Thank you, brave one,' she said gently, as she gave Laali some water and turned to face the other women.

'They are here, sisters. They have come to cut our trees and burn our forests,' she said, sombrely.

Everyone was frightened. They exchanged looks and murmured amongst themselves. They had been expecting this.

Rumour had it that their quaint little village of Reni, which had been surrounded by a thick forest for hundreds of years, was about to become a big town. The government wanted to turn this beautiful village into a city by building factories, hotels, houses and shops.

'There will be jobs and higher salaries, tourists will come and so will development,' the government had informed the villagers. But for the new buildings and structures to be constructed, the government had ordered all the trees to be cut and the land to be cleared.

So far, the villagers believed this was a rumour, but lived in fear that one day, people would come to destroy their quiet, beautiful forest home. Now that day had actually arrived.

All the men from their village had been tricked by the government into leaving a day in advance for the nearest big town. All those left in the village were women and little children.

'These men must be contractors who have been sent to hack the trees that have been home to us and our ancestors for hundreds of years,' said Gaura Devi. 'It is all part of their sinful plan,' she said, quietly.

More than 2,500 trees were going to be chopped in the following days, stripping the village of all its beauty and protection from natural disasters.

'Sinful because as humans, we are meant to protect Mother Earth, just as she protects us. Here in this village, we depend on these trees, on these shrubs, these herbs, fruits and flowers for our livelihood and for protection,' she continued. 'We must rise to protect her.'

'But how will we stop them, Gaura Devi?' cried one of the women. 'Who will listen to us?'

'Let's reason with them. After all, they are only humans, they will understand our plight,' said Gaura Devi, determined to change their minds.

But the women were in for a rude shock.

The contractors who were hired by the government arrived with huge axes for the trees and guns for the villagers. They brandished their weapons for everyone to see, threatening anyone from challenging their actions.

Gaura Devi and her small group of women were stunned. They had never even seen a gun before.

These men were in no mood for a discussion.

'They are threatening to kill anyone who tries to stop them,' murmured another woman in the group.

'If this is the language they speak, they will just have to learn a new one,' Gaura Devi said, determined.

She had a new plan.

She turned on her heels and marched to the village

square. There she knocked on each and every door, gathering support to protest against the beastly men.

Within just a few hours, twenty-seven women stood behind her in support.

The contractors had set up their tents where they would stay temporarily. They were about to begin work but what they saw, made them stop in their tracks.

Women and children of all shapes and sizes were throwing their arms around the trunks of trees, embracing them and standing silently, not moving, not speaking.

A tall, burly man with dishevelled hair and a bushy moustache came out of a big tent—he was the boss, the main contractor, who had come forward to see what the fuss was about.

'What in the world are you all doing, village idiots? Why are you coming in the way of our work? Don't you have anything better to do?' he was as puzzled as he was furious.

Gaura Devi finally spoke, her voice booming loudly, 'We are here to protest the killing of our trees. Go back to your bosses and tell them we will never let you harm our forest. This is our home; you cannot destroy it. We will not allow it.'

'What nonsense!' said the contractor, irritated. 'This is better for your village and for you villagers. You will have more jobs, more money and better development. Can't you see it is a good thing?'

'Then how come you want to kill our family? This forest is our mother and the trees are our family,' said Gaura Devi.

'I may not be educated or powerful, but I know this much. These trees are here for a reason—they have protected our village from the forces of nature such as storms, floods and even earthquakes. Cutting these trees can never be good for us,' she argued.

The contractor turned red in the face and said to his co-worker, 'These village bumpkins will not understand anything. They are just stupid. I guess I just have to deal with them how I know best,' he said menacingly, as he took his three-foot-long hunting gun out of its case.

The women and children behind Gaura Devi gasped. They couldn't believe the man was pointing a gun at a harmless, unarmed woman.

In response, she simply stepped in front of a tree and embraced it with both her hands.

'If you want to cut this tree, either shoot me or axe me down first,' she said. 'I will shield the tree until my last breath.'

'You know I will do it,' he shouted, pointing the gun straight at her.

The air was still, and the trees stood unruffled and unperturbed, much like Gaura Devi's spirit.

She wrapped her frail arms around the trunk of a hundred-year-old tree. As she closed her eyes and pressed her forehead against the rough bark, she felt a familiar connection with the tree. She had felt this before.

As an eight-year-old, Gaura Devi would accompany her mother to the forest to gather fruits and water from the nearby stream.

Her mother would say, 'Do you know, the roots of these trees hold this mountain together? They keep the soil from eroding down the hillside and washing our village away with the rains.'

'Hmmm. So, the roots are like hands that hold the Earth close together in a big, warm hug,' little Gaura Devi would say innocently. 'Like this?' she giggled, as she hugged a large tree as tightly as she could.

Mother would always laugh at her silly jokes and vivid imagination. She would sing an old village tune about trees. '*Maatu hamru, paani hamru, hamra hi chhan yi baun bhi...*(The soil is ours, the water is ours, ours are these forests...).'

'Are you done, woman? Can we begin our work now?' the contractor bellowed, as Gaura Devi snapped out of her thoughts.

'The sun is going to set soon, and we have wasted an entire day, thanks to your histrionics.'

'I told you, if you want to chop the tree, then chop me along with it,' she said, looking squarely into the burly man's eyes.

All twenty-seven women followed Gaura Devi's example, and each threw their arms around a tree.

They stood there unwavering, watching the moon rise into the sky, slowly slipping behind the clouds and illuminating the star-studded sky. They stood there, sat there and slept there, at the foot of the trees that seemed to stand guard all night long.

The next morning, as the men came out of their tents

to start work, they were astonished to see the women standing resolute, their arms still around the trees. One of the men was sent to the contractor's tent to inform him of the spectacle.

Outraged, the contractor screamed so loudly that the children, who were sitting next to their mothers, reeled back in horror. As the women tried to reassure their children, the contractor emerged from his tent, looking like a mad bull with bloodshot eyes.

'Foolish woman, you want to die?' he snarled at Gaura Devi. 'Do you all want to die?' He looked around, addressing the protestors.

No one moved.

'Fine by me. I am instructing my men to axe you down along with the trees, just as you wish,' he said, gesturing to his men. 'I have warned you enough.'

The women, frightened but resolute, looked at their leader for a sign. Gaura Devi remained silent. Even with the threat looming over their heads, she remained calm, head resting against the bark, eyes closed in meditation.

Once again, she recalled her mother singing to her in her tinkling, melodious voice, '*Hamra hi chhan yi baun bhi*...(Ours are these forests...).'

What was the second line of the song? She tried to focus, but her thoughts were interrupted again.

The contractor's men were now hurling insults and abuses at the women protestors. They came close enough to scream into their ears, but the twenty-seven women did not budge.

The women closed their eyes and tried to shut out the harsh words of the contractor and his men. The women and children could do nothing but pray the day was over, and the men retired, frustrated and defeated yet again.

They spent another night under the open sky, with what seemed like a million stars twinkling brightly, just for them. It was as if the gods were watching over them.

The next morning, the contractor came up with another idea to get rid of Gaura Devi.

'Let's talk,' he said to Gaura Devi, as she looked up at his formidable frame. She had barely any energy after leaning against the same tree for the third day in a row. Still, she was nowhere close to giving up.

For the first time, she saw something in the burly contractor's eyes—a glimmer of sympathy.

He spoke, trying his best to sound gentle, 'Look, we are just doing our jobs, woman. We have been hired to cut down these trees, and if we don't, we will lose our jobs. Why don't you understand? There are issues bigger than saving these mute trees from being cut.'

'No,' she answered softly, barely audible. 'I understand that you are just doing your jobs. But what you are unable to understand is that we are doing our jobs too. As humans. We cannot and will not allow the death and destruction of our environment.'

He heaved a heavy sigh and stepped back. She could tell he was about to burst in frustration.

'Very well, then. Deal with the consequences,' he said, as he sent word to the government officials in New Delhi.

Word of the protest had now reached other villages too. From twenty-seven, the number of protesters in the 'Chipko' movement rose to hundreds. Men and women from neighbouring villages joined this non-violent satyagraha (a non-violent movement first begun by Mahatma Gandhi).

Journalists, policemen, politicians now began to pour into the village. Gaura Devi, along with the protesters, refused to budge, hugging the trees tightly, like children clinging on to their mothers.

Finally, much to the relief of the community, the contractor and his men announced that they were ordered to retract from the village—the tree-felling was cancelled.

Even though a wave of relief washed over the village and the neighbouring communities, Gaura Devi was worried.

'What if they come back?' she wondered.

But when the Prime Minister announced a 10-year ban on cutting trees in the entire region, Gaura Devi and the protesters were truly happy with their victory.

When all the fanfare died down after the crowds had left, Gaura Devi ran to the tree she had hugged so tightly for three days and three nights and whispered something to it.

Laali, who was watching intently, asked, 'What did you say to the tree?'

Gaura Devi smiled and said, 'I finally remembered my mother's song.'

'*Maatu hamru, paani hamru, hamra hi chhan yi baun bhi... Pitron na lagai baun, hamunahi ta bachon bhi.*' (The soil is ours, the water is ours, ours are these forests. Our forefathers raised them, it's we who must protect them.)

Based on the true story of the Chipko Movement initiated by Gaura Devi in the village of Reni in Garhwal, Uttarakhand (1974).

10.
The Village Monster

A boy called Bansi lived with his father in a small village, surrounded by a thick forest. In a tiny shop built just under their house, they sold milk from their two cows, and eggs from their hens.

Nothing extraordinary ever happened in their sleepy little village, much to Bansi's disappointment. He loved reading books about adventure and action heroes. He would often pretend to be a brave hero who fought off thugs and bandits with his bare hands. Sometimes, he would return from the village school, all muddy and bruised after having wrestled an imaginary villain.

Father would always laugh and shake his head. 'Son, I have lived here all my life, and I can assure you, nothing exciting will ever happen in this village.'

His father, however, was soon to be proven wrong.

One morning, father and son woke up to the sound of loud wailing near their house. Laalu, a trader who lived down the road from their house, was sitting on his porch, crying loudly. A few passers-by stopped to ask him what had happened.

Bansi and his father stuck their heads out of the window upstairs which opened onto the main street, allowing them to see and hear everything without having to step out of the house.

The father-son duo heard Laalu saying, 'Last night, there was an intruder in my house. My backyard is destroyed, my banana trees are demolished and the whole house has been turned upside down!'

'But didn't you hear anything?' one of the villagers asked him.

'Yes, I did, but by the time I came downstairs, it was all over.'

'Maybe it was a thief?' said another.

'But nothing was stolen!' Laalu cried. 'This is the strangest part. I checked everything–my money is intact, and no valuables were taken.'

'That's strange indeed,' the crowd murmured. 'What was the motive?'

The villagers consoled the trader and the crowd dispersed, wondering what must have happened.

Father shrugged, thinking Laalu the trader had perhaps made some enemies in business who had come to destroy his house to smite him.

'It's probably a personal matter,' said Father. 'Don't look so frightened,' he laughed.

Bansi wasn't as frightened as he was curious. He wanted to know who or what had intruded into their neighbour's home. After all, Laalu lived just a few houses away, and the incident had happened right under their noses!

The village police had already made its rounds; the village panchayat had discussed the intrusion in detail and everyone had come to the same conclusion—it must have been a business rival who had ransacked Laalu's house.

Bansi, however, was convinced something else was going on. By sunset, he decided to carry out his own investigation.

He waited until his father was away. Fearing for his life, Laalu the trader had left to stay with his relatives for a few nights.

All Bansi had to do was jump the fence and hop into Laalu's backyard. He could see why it was so easy for the intruder to have entered the house.

Once inside, he switched on his little torch. The path that led to the backyard was in shambles and his six banana trees had been brutally cut in half. The kitchen utensils were strewn about, and the furniture was upside down.

'Nothing was stolen,' he whispered to himself in the dark. 'What did the intruder want?'

He walked up the stairs next and saw that the intruder had left the upper floor untouched.

Did he leave as soon as Laalu woke up? Did he find what he wanted and left?

It was getting late, and his father was supposed to return from work, so Bansi prepared to leave. Just before jumping off the courtyard wall, something in the bushes below caught his eye.

It was a large impression made in the soft mud next to the wall. It looked like a giant foot without toes, so large that it made Bansi tremble just thinking of the creature it belonged to.

'This is not a human being,' thought Bansi, trembling. 'What in the world is this?' he mumbled to himself in shock.

Who knew what lurked in the shadows? What if it was watching him all this time?

Bansi shuddered as he hurried to climb the wall. He ran across the street, raced upstairs to the bedroom and banged the window shut—the same one that faced the street.

That night seemed darker somehow. The moonlight cast strange shadows on the wall, which Bansi thought looked exactly like the shape in the mud.

He could barely sleep that night, imagining different kinds of toe-less monsters that may be lurking in his neighbourhood.

The next afternoon, on his way back from the market, he overheard a conversation among a large group of villagers.

'Did you hear what happened to the farmer's house last night?' he heard someone saying.

'Yes, his field was completely destroyed!' said another. 'The goats who were tied up outside the house were so scared, they kept stomping their feet and crying out for help. Wonder what they saw...' the man's voice quivered as it trailed off.

'Nothing was stolen, can you imagine?' someone added.

'But there was utter destruction and mayhem. I think it's a curse upon our village.'

Bansi was terrified, having heard of another intrusion in their village, strikingly similar to the one at Laalu's house. He hurried home to report to his father.

Father's lips were pursed, and his brows knit together in a deep frown. Obviously, Bansi had to tell him about his excursion to Laalu's house on the previous night in order to report the facts.

He was not happy.

'Father, I'm sorry, but I just had to do it. I was curious! This thing...whatever it is, man or monster or curse, it's ruining our peace, our village. We ought to find out what it is. It's our duty, isn't it?'

'No it is not! Why go looking for trouble unnecessarily? You think you are being a hero like the ones in your storybooks?' he asked. Bansi didn't dare answer.

'Just drink your soup and go to bed, young man. You will not venture out alone again, without permission. Do you understand?' His father's voice boomed loudly in their small, wooden home.

Bansi's father was a man of few words, but those words were always firm and powerful. All Bansi could do was nod and finish his dinner.

'It's their personal matter, not ours,' he said, concluding the discussion.

That very night, something happened that made it personal for Bansi and his father. Terror struck their own home.

It was 3 a.m. when Bansi was awoken abruptly by a noise outside their house. It sounded like something was moving right outside, its quick and heavy footsteps becoming louder by the second.

He sat bolt upright, trembling from excitement, wondering if he should wake his father.

Somehow, he found the courage to walk up to the window, which he had bolted tightly. He opened it quietly, trying not to make the latch creak and looked outside, wide-eyed, not knowing what to expect.

The wind was chilly, and it was completely dark. The only light was from the moon.

Bansi squinted and tried to focus. All of a sudden, there was a thunderous sound so close by that he felt it vibrate through his body.

CRASH KABOOM CLANG!

His heart skipped a few beats as his father came running to the window.

'The shop!' Father cried. 'It's in our shop!'

They ran downstairs in a hurry. The shop door had been flung open, the overhead light broken, and the chicken coop toppled. The poor birds were cackling wildly, frightened by what had happened.

To their dismay, Bansi and his father saw the day's eggs smashed on the floor and the milk spilt from the cans.

The cows were bellowing loudly now and one by one, the lights in all the neighbour's houses came on.

'What's going on, Dhami?' shouted one of their neighbours.

'What's the commotion?' yelled another.

Within minutes, the neighbours gathered around their shop, shocked to see the damage. There was no culprit in sight.

Bansi stepped aside, to peer into the shadows outside the shop.

Maybe it's hiding.

'Who's there?' he called bravely, even if his voice choked a bit.

The only reply was a soft whistle from the chilly wind. In the far distance, the dark forest looked even scarier—its pine trees looking like the jagged teeth of a giant monster.

The next morning, his father was unnerved enough by the incident to call a meeting of the village elders.

'Whatever it is, it only seems to strike at night,' said one of the villagers.

'I think it's a ghoul,' said a woman standing close by. 'Haven't you heard of ghouls roaming the forests at night? They hang upside down and pounce on humans passing by.'

Everyone just stared at her, not wanting to believe her, but not being able to resist the information.

'Again, nothing was stolen, and no valuables taken, right?' she asked. 'It's because the ghouls are looking for something—human flesh! They are blind as bats, but they can sense when humans are near.'

Father looked at her and shook his head. He was not one to believe in ghosts or ghouls.

'She does have a point,' said another villager. 'Why would someone...or something try to break into our homes and not steal anything? We must be the prize—we, humans,' he said, his voice shaking.

'Or a demon. Someone from the neighbouring village was telling us about a serpent-headed monster that emerges from the forest every fortnight. It's the size of a deodar tree and has these huge, toeless, flat feet...'

Bansi couldn't hear the rest. His heart stopped at 'toeless feet'.

Toeless feet. That's exactly what he had seen in the mud.

He exchanged a surreptitious look with his father who, in turn, gestured for him to be quiet. Only God knew what would happen if their suspicions were confirmed.

A local priest who was standing amongst the villagers said, 'I shall perform an elaborate ritual to appease the village deity and drive this evil spirit away!'

The crowd turned to him in awe.

'It's a curse upon our villages,' he cried. 'But I will take care of it.'

Father had had enough.

'We must catch the monster tonight, before it does any more damage or worse, before it finds the human flesh it's looking for. Let's collect all the weapons we can—anything we can use to attack,' he said.

The village elders huddled together, crafting a plan to trap the evil monster.

At 10 p.m. that night, the villagers went to their hiding spots to wait. They had blankets, spears, poisoned arrows, bricks and even broomsticks, just in case. After all, they didn't even know what they were about to attack.

As the time approached, Bansi begged his father to let him join.

'Absolutely not,' said his father firmly. 'You will stay in bed,' he ordered.

Bansi was wide awake in his bed as the clock struck ten. His heart thumped wildly. He knew something was going to happen and just couldn't sleep. After all, how could he close his eyes knowing a gigantic half-reptilian monster was lurking in their village, looking for their flesh?

But time passed by, the clock ticked away, and there was no sign of the monster.

'Perhaps it can sense that they're waiting for him tonight,' thought Bansi.

He eventually drifted off to sleep, but as soon as the clock struck three, he sat upright. He had heard it again!

CRASH BOOM CLANG!

This time, the sound came from the house opposite his. It was empty because his neighbours were away.

But the blind ghoul or the mutant monster wouldn't know that there was nobody inside that house. Bansi feared that it would come to his house again, after finding nobody next door. Bansi trembled, as he realized he was home alone.

He shut his eyes tightly and summoned his inner courage. He thought about the worst things that could possibly happen—if it was a beast, it would charge hungrily towards him, sniffing the human flesh on him. But, thought Bansi, he could use the creature's blindness to his advantage.

He could make it run into a tree and become unconscious, he could make it trip, breaking its bones, he could...

Suddenly, he was not scared any more. He opened his eyes and cried, 'You're done for, nasty monster.'

He sprinted downstairs, grabbing a long wooden pole on the way. He felt safe, knowing his father and the villagers were in hiding, waiting to pounce on the monster as soon as it appeared.

And sure enough, the villagers came charging towards the house. They had heard the noises too and together, they broke into the house. Six or seven men bravely tore into the house, ready to attack.

Bansi waited outside the house in rapt attention, waiting for the monster to appear, poised for battle with his long wooden pole.

CLANG CLANG BOOOOM!

The noises inside the house were becoming louder.

'Perhaps the monster spotted the men,' Bansi thought. He braced himself for attack, clenching his weapon tightly in his fists.

'It's there! It's getting away!' cried one of the men inside.

Suddenly, amidst the loud cries of men, the monster burst out of the house, straight towards Bansi!

There, under the full moon's light, Bansi came face-to-face with it.

Huffing and panting, its dotted chest was heaving, and its long, slender legs were wobbling. It wasn't until it looked directly up at Bansi with its large almond-shaped eyes, that Bansi realized what it was.

It was not a monster or a ghoul or a demon.

It was a young deer—a fawn, in fact!

Just then, one of the men flung a brick at the deer, hitting its hind leg. The fawn let out a loud yelp and, just as it was preparing to sprint, fell to the ground instead.

The villagers caught up to Bansi and the fawn, breathless after the chase. They saw the fawn and couldn't believe their eyes.

'So, this is the evil monster?' laughed one of the villagers, despite all the huffing and panting.

'Maybe he comes out of the forest every day to find food in the village,' said one man, aghast.

'Perhaps he always visits in the dark because deer have excellent night vision,' said another. 'And he must be afraid of humans, so he avoids coming to the village during daytime.'

'But the footprint?' Bansi asked from the back.

Father finally noticed him and gaped in surprise.

'Look at its hooves, son. No toes. Also, perhaps because it has been raining, the marks on the soil were exaggerated and made the footprint look a lot bigger than it was. Well, so much for the ghoul story!' laughed Father. 'We'll be sure to tell the priest tomorrow that his anti-ghost ritual finally worked!'

They laughed heartily.

Father helped the deer get back on its feet, and they all watched as it disappeared into the forest.

As for Bansi, he prepared himself for a severe scolding from his father but to his surprise, his father broke into a smile. He slapped his back saying, 'I'm proud of your courage, my boy. You were ready to fight a demon or a ghoul. You really are the hero our village deserves.'

The deer was never seen again, but stories of the 'village monster' who was vanquished on a full moon night are told even today.

11.
The Spring Song

It was the first week of April and the mountain birds were at their busiest, noisiest best.

Over the highest branches of an old oak tree, a multi-coloured monal (a bird of the pheasant family) was trying to persuade its new mate to join him in song. She, however, was distracted by a flock of gossiping flycatchers (a kind of bird) on the branch below, who had plenty to say about the silly blue thrush (a kind of flycatcher) who had woken them up with her shrill whistling.

Lower down on a branch of the same tree, were two quarrelling bulbuls (a kind of bird). If they were meant to be singing, they were terrible at it.

On the lowest branch sat one lone slate-headed parakeet (a kind of parrot), who was looking wearily at the chatter around him. He cocked his head from side to side, not wanting to join a conversation but at the same time, looking for some interesting company.

He was in luck, for just below him, under the shade

of the big oak tree, sat a young boy.

'He looks lost, poor boy,' the parakeet guessed. Dressed in a shirt too big and trousers too short, the boy looked tired. His ankles were swollen, his knees were bruised, and his bare feet were chapped from walking too much.

Little droplets of water trickled down the leaves, making it a slippery path for the parakeet to navigate but it hopped and skipped and fluttered until it was perched right above the boy's head.

'What brings you here this beautiful morning, pal?' the parakeet asked the boy.

The boy looked up and his eyes grew wide upon seeing a talking bird. He had heard of mystical birds in the oak forests of Kumaon that could speak to humans, but he had never met one before.

'I have lost my way to my village... I have been walking for hours. Could you...could you, maybe, guide me back? I live close to Kali-nadi, the black river. Do you know where it is?' he asked nervously.

'Oh, the black river! Of course I know where it is. I can guide you there,' the parakeet said, its eyes narrowing mischievously. 'But only on one condition.'

'What condition?' asked the boy.

'You will have to solve my riddles on the way!' replied the parakeet.

It was the first time the boy had seen a bird grinning.

'Oh, I am terrible at solving riddles. You will have to give me some clues, please,' the boy pleaded.

The parrot thought for a while and said, 'I am sure you

have heard the most famous song of Kumaon?'

'Bedu pakho (the figs have ripened)?' asked the boy.

'Of course,' replied the bird, happy that the boy knew his favourite song.

'I know it by heart. Everyone knows the spring song—we sing it just before harvest season,' cried the boy, excitedly.

'Very well then. You'll find all the clues to my riddles in the verses of the song,' said the parakeet, as he flew ahead of the boy as they began their long journey.

'This way!' the bird gestured. 'Listen carefully, bal (kid). Here's my first riddle. Look for clues in the first verse of the song.'

'I live in disguises four,

I love the rain and even the snow.

You can find me anywhere you go,

The Earth and the Sun will surely know.

What am I?'

The boy began to sing the first verse of the song, looking for a clue.

'*Bedu pakho, baad masa*

Bedu pakho, baad masa,

O Narain, kaphal pakho chaita, meri chaila.'

He thought aloud, 'The verse means, figs ripen throughout the year, but the kafal berry ripens only in spring.'

'There's a clue in the song, think carefully,' the parakeet prompted him.

'Season!' the boy exclaimed. 'The answer to the riddle is season.'

'Well done!' said the parakeet. 'Here's the next one.'
'You may never call her by her name,
But she has the sweetest names for you
All the same.
You may forget to thank her every now and then,
But you can be sure she'll save you
Even from a lion's den!
Who is she?'

The boy starts to sing the second verse of the song, looking for a clue.

'*Bhuna bhuna din ayo,*
Bhuna bhuna din ayo,
O Narain, bhuja teri maita, meri chaila.'

He said aloud, 'It means, the lovely warm days of spring are here. It's time to go to my mother's house.'

'Yes, that's the verse. Now look for a clue in it,' teased the parakeet.

The boy thinks for some time. 'Hmmm...let me see, is the answer, "mother"?' he asked the parakeet.

The parrot was delighted. 'You are a clever boy, the answer is mother, indeed! Let's see if you can guess another one.'

'People come from far and wide
Looking for peace and a divine guide.
Here, they offer fruits and flowers
In the hope for inner powers.
Which place is this?'

The boy sang the next verse of the song.
'*Almora ko Nanda Devi,*

Almora ko Nanda Devi

O Narain, phula chaduni pata, meri chaila'

'At the temple of Nanda Devi in Almora, people offer flowers and leaves,' the boy muttered to himself, hoping to find a clue.

The parakeet chuckled, 'The clue is so obvious, bal. Think, think!'

'Oh I know!' said the boy. 'It's a temple!'

The parakeet was impressed by the boy's wit. 'You are absolutely right! Now, answer the last riddle.'

'Fruits and flowers, berry and cherry,

Both look lovely in this hue.

Fresh tomatoes and the cheeks of children merry,

This is the colour of love that's true.

What colour is this?'

The boy sang again.

'*Almora ko Laal Bazaar,*

Almora ko Laal Bazaar,

O Narain, laal maati ki seedi, meri chaila.'

'This means the Lal Bazaar of Almora has stairs made out of red soil,' he thought out aloud.

'Yes, so what is the answer to the riddle?' asked the parakeet.

'Oh it's red, the colour red!' cried the boy.

'Well done!' exclaimed the parrot. 'And look, here we are, at the black river.'

The boy looked around, astonished. They had reached his village and were standing right beside the gurgling Kali-nadi, his home.

'Thank you, oh wise parrot,' said the boy, smiling. 'I was so busy singing the song and solving those riddles that I forgot all about how tired I was!'

He wondered if this had been the clever bird's plan all along.

The two friends bid farewell and parted ways, promising to meet again someday, under the same noisy, old oak tree.

12.
Haria's Kitchen

In a small village near Almora, lived a young boy named Haria. On his tenth birthday, his aunt and uncle offered, as a grand gift, to pay for his education in the big town.

Haria's parents were overjoyed because they couldn't afford the school fees but always wished for bigger and better opportunities for their son. Shy and obedient Haria agreed to go and live at his aunt and uncle's house in the town, even though he hated the idea of leaving his parents behind.

'One day, I'll take you to live with me in the big town, Ija and Babu,' he said to his parents before leaving. 'I'll work very hard in school, I promise.'

Things in the big town were a bit different from what he had expected.

The aunt and uncle who had seemed generous earlier, started making Haria do all their household chores. They kept him so busy with daily tasks that he didn't have any time to play outside or make friends in the neighbourhood.

His only solace was that they enrolled him in the big school, as promised.

In school, he tried hard to keep up with his studies, but found the lessons very difficult. Everything was new and different and Haria felt lonely and misunderstood.

Back home, his aunt would make him buy vegetables from the market, wash the dishes, clean the stable and tend to the large herb garden in their backyard.

Haria started to hate his life in the big town. He really wanted to go back home to his village.

One day, just after his trip to the vegetable market, Haria began to feel very hungry. His aunt and uncle were away for the day, and there was nothing to eat in the house.

Helpless and hungry, Haria began to boil some water and he put a small portion of rice in it. He also pounded some mustard seeds together, grated some cucumber and added it to a little yogurt along with a pinch of turmeric.

'Ah! My favourite raita,' he said, smiling as he tasted it. 'Now what shall I eat with the rice?' he wondered.

He rubbed his palms together and checked the vegetable basket he had just brought back from the market—radish, pumpkin and spinach. He knew he would get a sound scolding if his aunt found any vegetable missing, so he took care to use very small quantities.

Within an hour, Haria had cooked up an entire feast for himself with his native dishes—there was kafuli, a yam dish made with spinach, mooli techwa, a spicy preparation made out of radish, and chainsoo, a soup made out of some leftover grains in storage.

The house was filled with the aroma of garlic, mustard and spicy herbs which Haria had picked from the backyard. After all, Haria had been nibbling on the herbs and learning about their flavours each day, as he watered and pruned the plants in the backyard.

He relished the dishes one by one, licking his fingers and wishing for more, but it was time for his aunt and uncle to come back home. He promised himself he would make some more as soon as he got the chance.

To his delight, he learnt that his aunt and uncle were going away for a week to a relative's house in the neighbouring village.

'Make sure all the chores are done exactly the way I like them,' his aunt said sharply. 'You will make your own food, yes? Otherwise, there are plenty of fruits in the house to survive on,' she shrugged.

'I have asked the neighbour to keep an eye on you, so you best behave, boy!' Uncle added.

Haria nodded happily.

The boy cooked as if it were his only escape—he chopped, he pureed, and he fried. He snipped, he peeled, and he pounded until the entire neighbourhood was fragrant with the aromas coming from the house.

The next day, he decided to pack some food for school as well. This time, he made a scrumptious curry of bhatt beans with jhangora for dessert, a sweet dish made out of millet grains.

As soon as he opened his lunch box at school, he found a familiar face looking down at him. It was his classmate,

Bhimu, one of the naughtiest and most gregarious boys in class.

'What have you got there, new boy?' he asked, peeking into his box.

'It's...it's nothing,' replied a petrified Haria, frightened of being confronted by the big and handsome Bhimu.

'Then how come "nothing" smells so good?' laughed Bhimu, plonking down beside him.

'It's just something I made in a hurry; you may taste it, but I don't know if you'll like...' even as Haria trailed off, Bhimu took his lunchbox in his own hands and took a large bite.

'What in the world!' exclaimed Bhimu. He was chewing slowly, as if he didn't ever want the taste in his mouth to vanish.

'You made this?'

'Uh, yes. Is it all right?'

Bhimu looked like his eyes were going to pop out of their sockets. 'It's the best thing I have ever eaten in my entire life!' he cried. 'Please, please, may I have some more?'

Haria gladly shared his lunch with his new friend.

Every day, Haria would make something to share at lunch. Stories about his delicious food spread so far that the headmaster came around to sample the fare one day.

'It is the best chainsoo I have ever tasted,' he declared. 'Coming from a ten-year-old!' he shook his head, amazed.

Encouraged by the praise from his classmates and headmaster, Haria decided to surprise his aunt and uncle too.

He toiled hard in the kitchen, grating and tossing, straining and slicing. The steam from the kitchen rose high in the air, making even the cows in the stable restless and hungry.

When they came back, his aunt and uncle were stunned after the very first bite of the yam kafuli. Haria mistook their silence for anger.

'I am sorry I used the kitchen ingredients and vegetables without asking you,' he stammered an apology.

'NO, NO,' his aunt was the first to speak. 'This is brilliant! Who knew we had a brilliant cook in our very own home?' she exclaimed, stroking his hair and making him sit at the table with them—both of which she had never done before.

'I am never making food again in this house,' she said, and she meant it. 'Haria will make all our food from now on.'

Uncle nodded at her and said, 'Oh wait, I have an excellent idea.' His eyes sparkled as he spoke.

'Why don't you cook for us and we'll start a small business—a home kitchen and a small restaurant!' he smiled in triumph, as if he had discovered electricity.

'But my school? I have to go to school every day. How will I cook in a restaurant?' asked Haria.

'What school?' Uncle stared coldly at Haria. 'Why waste your time there when you have such an incredible talent which can start making us money right away?'

Suddenly, Haria felt his mouth go dry, and his head started to spin.

'Oh no! What have I done? Now they will make me quit

school and stay at home to cook for them like a slave,' he thought in despair.

Sure enough, that's exactly what happened.

In the days that followed, Aunt and Uncle didn't allow Haria to go to school.

'Young man, let me tell you something,' said his aunt in a cool voice. 'We won't pay your school fees, so you can't go anyway. What you can do is start making food to sell so you can earn some money. We will manage the money until you are old enough to handle it though. Maybe for another 8-9 years or so.'

Haria stared at her in shock as she tried to hide a crooked smile.

'8 or 9 years?' Haria felt his knees go weak. He thought of Ija and Babu and how disappointed they would be if they found out he had dropped out of school.

'What are you staring at? Now get to work, boy!' his aunt hissed.

In the meantime, Haria's classmates, especially Bhimu, were very worried. It had been two weeks since Haria attended school. Bhimu missed the mouth-watering delicacies, but he missed his shy classmate even more. He decided to speak about Haria's absence to the headmaster.

'No one knows where he is, sir,' he told the headmaster. 'Maybe something bad has happened to him.'

'Yes, he was regular with his attendance so far. This is very strange. Let's go to his house tomorrow,' said the headmaster.

The next afternoon, after school, Bhimu and the

headmaster set out to look for Haria at his uncle's house. As soon as they spotted the house, they stopped in their tracks, not believing the scene before their eyes.

A small shed had been constructed as an extension to Haria's aunt and uncle's gaudy yellow house. Three tables and a few chairs had been crammed into the tiny space. A small board on the gate of the shed read, 'Haria's Kitchen.' Each table was occupied with customers.

'What in the world?' Bhimu blurted out.

They entered the restaurant, hoping to catch a glimpse of Haria.

Suddenly, they saw Haria approaching them from behind a curtain that led to the kitchen.

'Haria! Where have you been? Why have you not come to school for two weeks? What is all this?' Bhimu gestured towards Haria's crumbled shirt and messy hair. Haria's eyes were dull, and he looked exhausted.

Haria didn't answer any of his questions. Instead he asked, 'What would you like to have? We have Kumaoni special dishes, but we also make dishes on request.' Haria uttered these words as if he had rehearsed them over and over again.

'Stop it Haria!' exclaimed Bhimu. 'Don't pretend to not recognize us! You have been missing school for this? Waiting tables and making food in this restaurant?'

Haria looked up directly at their faces for the first time. His eyes were now clouded with tears and he whispered, his lips trembling, 'Please forgive me. I had to leave school and work here under the orders of my aunt and uncle. They want me to cook and run this restaurant. I have to do this now.' He hung his head low, his whole body shaking.

Bhimu was speechless. The headmaster put a hand on Haria's shoulder and said, 'This is not right. We will do something, don't worry. Let's think about how to get you out of here.'

'It's too late,' said Haria, shaking his head. 'They will never let me go now. They have stopped paying my school fees.'

Just then, Bhimu spotted Haria's aunt and uncle approaching. He nudged the headmaster and gestured for them to leave immediately. They didn't want Haria to get in trouble.

'Listen, I have an idea. We have to leave now, but we will come here tomorrow around the same time, pretending to be customers—keep a table free for us,' whispered Bhimu, as he scampered away.

Haria wiped his tears and nodded.

As soon as they were out of earshot, Bhimu said, 'Sir, I don't know if you will agree with this plan, but we have no other choice.'

'Go on, boy,' said the teacher, willing to try anything for Haria.

'There are a few herbs that can be found on the far end of that hill,' he said, pointing eastwards towards a few small hillocks. 'All we need is a bunch of those particular herbs and leaves—I promise you we can rescue Haria, using just those herbs.'

'How? Which herbs are you talking about?' asked the headmaster puzzled.

A mischievous smile crept upon his lips. 'I can only show you that tomorrow, sir,' said Bhimu.

The next day, as promised, Bhimu and the headmaster reached 'Haria's Kitchen' after school, pretending to be hungry customers. The restaurant was packed once again. When Haria approached their table to take their order, Bhimu quietly slipped a small cloth bag under the table, nudging him to take it from him.

Haria grabbed the cloth bag and ran to the kitchen, making sure no one saw what he had smuggled inside.

He was fiddling with the strings of the bag with trembling fingers when something stung him sharply.

'OUCH! Has Bhimu gone mad? I think there's a scorpion in there!' Haria cried, alarmed.

But the bag didn't move at all.

Slowly, Haria approached the cloth bag again and then he knew exactly what he was looking at. 'Bichoo ghass!' he cried.

It was no scorpion, but it sure stung like one. Sitting innocently in the bag was a big bunch of nettle leaf, called bichoo ghass, the kind that stings like a scorpion, and which can make a person itch for hours. There was also another smaller pouch, full of strange-looking yellow seeds.

He peeked out of the kitchen to look at Bhimu and the headmaster. Bhimu was gesturing for him to toss the leaves and seeds into the food he was making for his customers.

With his heart thumping wildly in his chest, Haria tossed all the strange yellow seeds in the fresh food.

AAACHOOOO!

Haria sneezed so loud and hard, he felt his muscles loosen up.

He had to fashion a hand glove out of a kitchen cloth to handle the bichoo ghass as he rubbed it all over the utensils. He even put a few leaves as decorations on some of the dishes. Then he walked out to serve the food as if nothing had happened.

In less than two minutes, there was absolute chaos.

The room exploded into a flurry of people sneezing and itching uncontrollably, not knowing whether to itch first or finish sneezing.

There were customers lying on the floor trying to scratch their backs while others had started to rub themselves on the barks of trees. Some were trying to scratch their backs while sneezing and were failing miserably at both activities.

Bhimu couldn't control his laughter.

Soon, Haria's aunt and uncle rushed into the kitchen to see what's happening and accidentally brushed past the nettle leaves on the kitchen countertop. Uncle was furious to see what was happening to his customers and insisted on tasting the food to find out what was wrong with it. As soon as he did, he was taken over by a violent bout of sneezes.

'Youuuu ACHOO! Jah-jah-just ACHOOOOOO wait! Sa-sa-scoundrel ACHOOO! What the ha-ha-hell ACHOOO?' Uncle tried to scold Haria, but he looked so comical bent over trying not to sneeze, that Haria started to giggle too.

His aunt tried to get hold of Haria's ear to twist it but alas! All she could do was scratch her own back, even scraping against the wall for some relief.

The house and kitchen looked like a circus.

'We wa-wa-will ACHOOOOO shut down this ka-ka-kitchen ACHOOOO!' some of the customers cried.

'Let's tear this pa-pa-place ACHOOOO down,' they said, and they did.

By the time the last customer left, the restaurant was completely torn down, the utensils broken. Haria's aunt and uncle tried to sit down, still scratching and sneezing, trying to make sense of what had happened.

'You scoundrel, you were better off in school. You ruined our business, foolish boy,' Uncle scolded Haria after his sneezing had subsided. 'You are going to pay for this!' he said menacingly.

The headmaster who had been waiting outside stepped in. He addressed Haria's aunt and uncle. 'As a customer, I will complain to the police and health authorities that you tried to poison your guests with bad food. Since the restaurant is run by you, out of your own home, you will be jailed!'

'What! NO! Please, please don't do this to us,' cried Uncle and Aunt, falling to his feet.

'All right, I won't complain on one condition—pay Haria's school fees and let him attend school. From this day onwards, he will have enough time for homework and play, and you will not burden him with chores.'

Uncle and Aunt nodded.

'If I hear even one complaint from Haria...'

'No, no you won't, sir. We agree to your condition,' they said.

And just like that, Haria was back in school the next day, bringing his friends the finest of his culinary delights.

He practised his cooking skills every single day to realize his dream of running his own restaurant and to come a few steps closer to bringing his Ija and Babu to the big town someday.

13.
Kafal

It was the saddest day of her life—the day her mother died.

The little princess, Phool Kumari remembered the day clearly. She had been out with her dear friends, the cowherds and goatherds of Genali. They were picking ripened kafal berries from wild shrubs and skipping happily in time to the beat of the damau drum.

Colourful wooden masks covered their faces, as they sang about the harvest season, skipping down the sloping terrace farms together.

The taste of the sweet-sour kafal was still fresh in her mouth when she returned home to the palace grounds. Something was wrong, she could sense it.

The palace was in mourning. Her father, the king took her aside to give her the terrible news. He was sobbing too.

'As you know, dear one, your mother was suffering from an illness for a long time. She is no more,' the king said, quietly.

Tears filled up Phool Kumari's eyes until she couldn't see any more.

The memory was still so fresh in her mind that it brought tears to her eyes every time she thought about her mother.

She looked out of the window of the palace tower where she could see the goatherds and cowherds playing in the far distance–friends that she had abandoned since that day. They would often look up and wave to her, but she never waved back.

She remembered how her mother would make all of them sit under a tree in the meadow and tell stories that made them laugh. Mother even had a fat little goat called Rampu, who would topple over his own feet because he was too fat. Oh, how they laughed every time he tripped!

But the princess didn't smile, not even while remembering this. She might have even forgotten how to smile since that day.

The king was worried. Two years was a long time, but his daughter was still immersed in sadness.

All he wanted to do was make her smile again and the thought consumed him day and night. He appealed to his ministers for help, but no one could offer a remedy.

The king had vowed to do everything in his power to help the princess cheer up again. 'What would you like, my love?' he offered. 'You can ask for anything.'

The sad princess just looked at her feet and shook her head, for she only longed for her mother.

Finally one day, he decided to make an announcement

in his kingdom.

'Hear! Hear! Hear!' announced the king's messengers. 'Whoever makes the princess smile will be handsomely rewarded by the king. A contest will be held at the palace grounds, next week.'

The messengers travelled far and wide across the mountains of Kumaon. Market squares, villages, farms and forests—they went everywhere to spread the word. They wanted every single person in the kingdom to hear the message and help the princess cheer up.

When Phool Kumari heard about this contest, she was shocked, even a bit angry that her father had announced this without speaking with her.

He didn't know that meeting people made her nervous these days. She hated attention from people and now her father had announced some sort of a circus just for her.

'Please Father, I beg you not to do this. You don't understand...' is all she could say to explain, tears welling up in her eyes again.

'No, darling, let me do this—for you and me both,' he said firmly.

She agreed sadly, but only out of love for her father.

On the day of the contest, people gathered at the palace grounds in large numbers. The palace was decorated with colourful banners, festoons and glittering lights.

The happy faces and festivities made poor Phool Kumari think of happier times in the palace, with her mother. It made her all the more miserable.

All kinds of entertainers showed up and so did a large

crowd of villagers from far and wide—farmers, blacksmiths, vendors—everyone came to watch.

'Who will make the princess smile?' people murmured in excitement.

Phool Kumari sat in her chamber by the window, only with her father by her side.

The first contestant came with a monkey which performed its tricks. It juggled six balls at a time and even stole treats out of his master's hand. The spectators laughed and clapped. The monkey did somersaults to acknowledge the happy crowd.

The princess, however, was not amused. She looked on from her chamber, still dull and sad.

Next came a poet, who told his jokes in limericks and sang songs with funny lyrics. The crowd loved it and threw their hands up in appreciation.

Still, there was no response from the princess. She simply couldn't wait for the contest to get over, so she could go back to her room and sleep.

Even the magician who pulled a bird out of an empty pot and made a chicken hatch an orange, couldn't cheer her up. He even took a mouse out of his ear, just for the princess' sake. The crowd howled and hollered for more, but she was still sad as ever.

The king was beginning to lose hope.

Just then, a giant goat with a large, jiggling belly stumbled onto the stage. His belly was so big that he kept tripping over his own feet.

Phool Kumari suddenly sat bolt upright, her eyes fixed

on the goat.

A little boy began to play the damau drum in the background, while the giant goat began dancing to the beat with great gusto. The crowd laughed and cheered him on.

The goat appeared to be encouraged by all the cheering and started to dance faster and faster. The beats picked up pace and soon the goat was dancing with gay abandon. He looked like a spinning top that was about to topple over at any moment.

He danced faster and faster until all of a sudden, his humongous tummy fell to the ground with a loud thud.

The princess gasped and then burst into peals of laughter that echoed around the palace. The crowd was howling, but the king was simply astonished to see his daughter happy again. He turned to take a closer look at the goat and realized it was a disguise!

The goat's tummy was made from mud and hay, so the glue gave way and it fell off. Inside the goat's disguise was a boy, looking sheepish and shy. He looked up and waved to the princess.

Puzzled, the king looked at his daughter for an explanation.

Phool Kumari was laughing heartily and waving back. She laughed until there were tears in her eyes.

She turned to the king and said, 'Father, that boy in the goat's disguise is good old Gopi, my friend from the meadows, and this was the story of Mother's clumsy goat, the one she used to tell us every day. What was his name? Er...Rampu!' she said brightly, her eyes twinkling.

'We used to sing harvest songs every year during the Hil Jatra festival, wearing the masks. Look, Gopi painted a mask that looks just like Rampu!'

Father and daughter hugged each other and laughed and cried together.

Gopi, the goatherd, was handsomely rewarded, as promised.

With the prize money, he built a beautiful house for his goats and named it 'Phool Kumari' after the lovely princess.

The princess reunited with her friends from the meadows and with Rampu who had been living with Gopi all along. Phool Kumari was happy to see he was still as clumsy as when she had last seen him.

The cowherds offered her freshly picked kafal. It was that time of the year again. As Phool Kumari tasted the familiar sour-sweet flavour of the fruit, she remembered her mother and this time, she smiled.

From that day onwards, Gopi narrated one of the Queen Mother's stories every single day, much to the delight of the happy princess.

14.
A Night in the Dark Forest

Everything about the old sage from Dharchula looked strange and frightening.

This man had been travelling across the peaks and valleys of Kumaon, his brow drenched in sweat and the soles of his feet cracked from walking. Nobody knew where he was coming from or where he was going, and no one dared to ask him. It just didn't seem like a good idea to come in his way.

His silver dreadlocks were coiled high on his head and his matted beard was tied into a large knot which dangled loosely under his chin. Black shadows circled his eyes and his eyeballs seemed to bulge out of their sockets. He looked like a madman.

Wherever he went, children scampered out of his way, startled by his appearance.

But not brave Bhula. This curious boy darted out of his door as soon as he saw the man passing the lane of his house.

'Who are you? What brings you here?' Bhula called loudly after the man had walked a few paces ahead.

Much to the boy's horror, he stopped in his tracks, turned back and started walking straight towards him.

The boy gulped but stood his ground. 'We have never seen you here before. Are you visiting someone's house? Maybe I can help you with an address?'

He had so many more questions.

What was in his jhola (loosely hanging bag)? Did he carry a weapon in it? How long had he not cut his hair? Did he want to grow it until it swept the ground behind him?

He only dared to ask him the first question.

The old man's large, bulgy eyes suddenly crinkled into what must have been a smile. Bhula could not see the man's mouth because of his big, messy moustache and beard.

'I am just passing through this village in order to get to the Dark Forest. I plan to reach before sunset,' he said, with a quick nod. 'So long then,' he said, hurrying along the lane.

Bhula was stunned into silence.

'The Dark Forest,' he whispered under his breath, shuddering. 'He's actually going to the Dark Forest.'

The forest, which lay just beyond the boundary of this village, was known to hold unspeakable secrets. It was, well, very, very dark and teeming with dangerous predators and mysterious, forbidden types of plants—the kinds that could kill a human within minutes. Legend had it that whoever ventured into the Dark Forest, either returned a changed person, or never returned at all.

Bhula darted behind the old man.

'But why? Why would you willingly go into the Dark Forest? Surely you must know it's extremely dangerous.'

The sage sighed and spoke slowly, 'I must go to meditate and offer penance, child. I need the answer to a question that has been troubling me all my life.'

Young Bhula couldn't contain his curiosity. 'What question?'

As the man looked at little Bhula's face, with his wide eyes and his perky ears, he didn't have the heart to ask him to leave him alone.

'How can we put an end to evil in this world?' the man replied.

'There must be some force, some weapon, some entity that can put an end to evil thoughts and actions. I am going to find out what it is,' he said, looking frightfully determined.

Bhula tried his best to understand what he had just said, as the man disappeared around the bend of the lane and stepped into the deep, dark ravines of the forest. He hoped he would see the old man again, somehow, even though his chances of surviving a night in the Dark Forest seemed very slim.

One look at the sage's frail, reed-thin body and his flimsy dhoti made Bhula shake his head.

The forest had received its name for a reason. Sunlight never touched the ground there, as the thick canopy of trees blocked the light completely. Thick roots protruded from the ground, making it jagged and difficult to walk on.

The sage stumbled in the darkness. The path was not

easy to navigate and would become even more dangerous, should a man-eater catch his trail.

He walked for hours, deeper and deeper into the forest, until he reached an enchanting lagoon, filled with lotuses. A few rays of light that managed to sear through the trees reflected off the water, illuminating the lagoon in a beautiful, soft glow.

This was the spot the sage chose as his temporary home. He sat comfortably on the small mat, which he took out of his jhola, along with a small bracelet of beads, closed his eyes and sank into meditation.

It was silent there, aside from the call of a wild bird in the distance or the shuffling of leaves nearby. The air was so still that the smallest sound could make one jump out of one's skin.

The night set in quickly and the forest plunged into pitch darkness.

Slowly, a low hum began to emanate from the lotus pond. The hum grew louder and louder until it was almost deafening. A swarm of insects, large and menacing, rose above the water like a blood-thirsty battalion, finding its way towards the sage.

The swarm attacked the old man, with what felt like a hundred tiny arrows piercing his skin. The old man could feel the sharp sting on his skin, his flesh beginning to swell from the piercings.

He continued to meditate, painfully aware of what was happening to him, and didn't move a muscle.

Nearby, a hungry bear was on the prowl. The bear followed the noise made by the swarm of insects, sensing the possibility of prey and saw the old man sitting still.

Grunting, he picked up his pace and was soon standing within inches of the sage, sniffing, snarling and growling in the old man's face.

'He is so very still,' the bear thought. 'Could he be dead?' he wondered, sniffing the sage one last time as he walked away. After all, bears don't scavenge for dead meat, not even at their hungriest.

The swarm of mosquitoes had been driven away by the bear, and the bear himself had now lost interest. All this while, the sage sat steadfast in his meditation.

What no one noticed till then was a pair of eyes watching the scene from behind the tall grass across the lagoon—the fiery eyes of a man-eating tiger, waiting to pounce on a sitting prey.

The soft mud sank under the weight of the tiger's heavy limbs, his claws were drawn in attack and his teeth gnashed in anticipation. The tiger steadily advanced towards the man who sat still, oblivious to the sound of the tiger's paws thumping in the marsh.

As soon as the tiger stepped out of the grass and prepared to pounce, he saw something that made him stop in his tracks—it was the one thing that agitated tigers the most—a long, poisonous snake.

HISSSSSSSS

'Back off, tiger! He's mine,' hissed the snake who had, by now, coiled its undulating body around the old man's neck and shoulders.

'Be gone, unless you want to die from my poisonous bite—a very, very slow and painful death,' the snake warned the tiger.

She hissed again. The tiger detested that sound.

'This prey is mine, and I shall have him all to myself,' the snake hissed a final warning.

The tiger backed away, not wanting to risk a poisonous

bite for a man that looked all skin and bones.

'Hardly any meat there, anyway,' thought the tiger.

Just as the snake was about to tighten its grip around the sage, a large vulture came gliding down, scooped up the writhing body of the snake and took off with a giant flap of its wings, all in one fell swoop.

The snake struggled to break away mid-air, but the vulture had its prey in an iron grip. It was hungry too, after all.

The sage breathed a heavy sigh of relief, still in meditation. He knew if he had struggled earlier, the snake would have only coiled around tighter and faster, and killed him sooner.

Perched on the branches of the tree nearby, the vulture shared the big meal with its mate.

It was almost dawn now.

The sage sat in the same spot, still as stone, but with a gentle smile on his face.

As soon as the sun rose and wrapped the lagoon in its soft light, the wise man knew it was time. He opened his eyes.

His penance done, he pulled out a small bottle of oil from his jhola, along with a comb, a pair of large scissors and a shaving blade.

He walked out of the Dark Forest, with his short-cropped hair and clean-shaven handsome face glowing in the morning sun, a changed man indeed.

As he approached the village, he was surprised to find a small crowd of villagers cheering for him. Bhula, the same boy he had met earlier, was looking visibly happy and relieved, though astonished at the man's new avatar.

'You made it, welcome back!' he exclaimed happily. 'But did you find the answer to your question, brave man? How can you conquer all evil in the world?'

'Yes, I did,' smiled the old man. 'And no, you can't.'

His sparkling eyes crinkled once again, laughing as he saw the puzzled looks on the villagers' faces, especially Bhula's, who was scratching his head, trying to understand.

'I realized I can do nothing to conquer evil. But I can conquer my own mind,' he explained, as he remembered the events of the night.

'How?' asked the curious boy.

'By simply keeping my own thoughts positive, steadfast and sincere, my actions will follow suit. No evil can ever harm me then,' said the wise man, flashing a smile at Bhula. 'If I had reacted with fear or anger to any of the things that happened to me last night, I would have succumbed to evil myself.'

Bhula nodded, as the wise old man walked across the lane in front of his house and disappeared into the horizon.

15.
Holi

It was the morning of Holi, the festival of colours, and the tiny village near Kausani was celebrating the festival in full swing. It was only 9 in the morning but everyone was already covered in bright hues of yellow and blue, pink and orange.

The smell of freshly made singhal (spiral-shaped sweet bread), rose high in the air as a troupe of men in bright outfits twirled in a circle, brandishing their swords. They jabbed the air with their swords in one hand, and with the other, they kept their iron shields close to their bodies while moving their feet in tune to the beat of the dhol and damau drums.

Bhola had never seen men like these before. His mouth fell open, 'What in the world...?' he wondered aloud, watching the sword fight, inches away from him.

'They are called Choliyas—they dance at weddings and other occasions,' said Bhaguni, his neighbour and friend, who always seemed to know about such obscure things. She was standing beside him, clapping her hands in glee.

'But with swords? These men are twirling their swords like spinning tops in the air! What if they hurt someone?' Bhola asked, alarmed at the speed at which these Choliyas were moving.

'Silly you!' Bhaguni giggled, her laughter sounding like tinkling bells. 'Are you scared?'

'No, of course not, I was just saying...' Bhola attempted to explain, but she cut him off.

'You know, you ought to have courage. You never know when it comes in handy,' she added. 'By the way, you don't have to worry about the Choliya dancers. They are skilled in their dance form and they practise for hours. I heard Father say that thousands of years ago, Kumaoni soldiers called Khasas would perform this dance at weddings to protect the bride and groom from evil spirits and even demons. These Choliya dancers are simply taking that tradition forward.'

'HAPPY HOLI!'

Suddenly, there was a hard slap on Bhola's back.

'To you too, Kanu,' Bhola said, greeting his friend. He had a pouch of blue-coloured powder in his palm and dabbed some of it on his friend's right cheek.

'And, to you too!' Kanu laughed as he smeared Bhaguni's face in bright yellow colour.

By the time they were done playing, it was mid-afternoon and patches of blue, pink, yellow and purple covered their faces and bodies completely.

'Why, I can barely recognize you!' cried Chandu, the milkman, as he passed by on his cycle.

'Water, I need water!' said Bhaguni. 'But If I go home now, mother will force me to clean up and I won't be able to come out and play anymore.'

'Me too!' said Kanu.

'All right, let's go to the lake on the other side of the hill, then. There's plenty of drinking water and we can all come back to play some more,' Bhola said, happy with his idea.

As they made their way between the thick bushes and a tall patch of trees that surrounded the lake, they heard a strange rustling sound, not far from where they were.

CRUNCH! CRUNCH!

They could hear the sound of leaves shuffling near them. As far as Bhola knew, this shortcut to the lake was always completely deserted, and yet, they were not alone.

Bhaguni tugged at his elbow and whispered, 'Let's go back!'

'Don't worry, it must be a small animal,' Bhola whispered back. 'The lake is just around the corner, come!' he gestured for them to follow him.

They hadn't taken many steps further when he looked back to see Kanu trailing away. He was walking in the direction of the rustling sound! Before Bhola could signal at him to stop, Kanu had hidden himself behind a large trunk of a tree.

Kanu gestured for them to join him, one hand on his lips and the other waving at them.

Bhaguni and Bhola shrugged, thinking if Kanu was brave enough, so were they. They each took position behind a tree next to Kanu, and squinted in the direction of the noise.

'I can't see anything,' said Bhaguni, training her eyes to focus on the narrow gap between the bushes.

'It's a hand cart. Look!' whispered Kanu. 'I just saw a part of it.' He pointed a finger towards a gap in the bushes.

A hand cart? In the middle of this lone hill?

Just then they heard a man's voice, 'This is good enough, I guess. We got television sets, some jewellery and cash. It was such a clean sweep, and so easy!'

They squinted to see a man speaking. He had messy hair which fell around his shoulders and arms so big, they could've belonged to a gorilla. He was looking down at a hand cart full of goods and appeared to be speaking to someone.

Another man could be partially seen between a gap in the trees, 'Hehe! Those idiotic villagers will be dumbstruck once they return to their homes to find everything gone. Just imagine the looks on their faces!' He was much neater in appearance, with short cropped hair and a colourful shirt.

'Load the last set!' said a third man. His voice was calm and heavy, and he was short and bald. 'He's probably their leader,' thought Bhola.

Bhaguni and Kanu scrambled behind another tree, closer to the action.

Bhola whispered as he shuffled his feet, eager to abandon their water-fetching mission and run back to the village, 'So, they are three bandits!'

'Make that four,' a raspy voice said from behind them, as they turned slowly. 'Spying on us, ha? You pesky kids are going to regret coming here,' growled the burly stranger, as he stepped towards the children.

Bhaguni and Kanu were too shocked to scream. The man was six feet tall and built like an ox. Bhola kept quiet because he understood that if they yelled out aloud, they would only alert the other thieves and soon be easily outnumbered.

Just as the burly bandit was about to grab all three of them with a single muscular arm, Bhola jabbed his hand in his pocket and took out a fistful of coloured powder. Before the burly man could react, Bhola thrust the coloured powder at his face, right under his nose and into his eyes, sending him reeling back.

That gave Bhaguni the chance to jab him with her elbow while Kanu stomped hard on the big man's feet. As the bandit wailed in pain, the three friends ran towards the village, only to hear the other men following them, close on their heels.

They ran downhill as fast as they could, stumbling and sliding down towards the village. They didn't have far to go because they could hear the trumpets and drumming from the Choliya procession, which seemed to be in full swing now.

'They are coming after us!' Kanu managed to shout while running at full speed.

'Turn right! Now! The temple! Hide!' shouted Bhaguni,

as they took a sharp detour and went rolling down the hill, one after another.

Luckily, the men didn't see them roll away. They continued running past them, straight towards the village.

'If they catch hold of us, I don't know what they will do to us,' Kanu said, huffing and puffing.

'We have to alert our parents somehow,' Bhaguni added.

'Yes, but how will we find them in the crowd?' asked Bhola, pointing to the festivities. 'We have to think of another plan in the meantime. The bandits are in the middle of the village now.'

'Oh wait! Let's clean all of this colour off our faces—they'll have trouble recognizing us then. If Chandu, the milkman, who sees us every morning, couldn't recognize us covered in Holi colours, then these men will definitely not be able to tell us apart without the colours!'

'Great idea! We should split up too, so they will find it harder to track us,' said Bhaguni.

Bhola remembered how thirsty Bhaguni had been and how they still hadn't had any water. He looked around the temple for water but there was nothing to drink.

Bhaguni went to inform the police about the robbery, Kanu went looking for their parents and Bhola had the task of keeping track of the bandits in the crowd.

As they entered the crowd separately, the sounds of the trumpets and beating of the drums became louder. Bhola craned his neck to look for the bandits in the crowd but the rows of men and women obstructed his view.

The Choliya dancers were moving with even more

fervour and grace. The procession was reaching a crescendo and the crowd was swelling by the minute.

Bhola managed to climb a low wall at the edge of the ground and perched himself carefully over a wall in order to spot the thieves.

After scanning the crowd for a long time, Bhola finally spotted them—the man with the long, unruly hair, one with the colourful shirt, the short and bald one and the burly six-foot tall man.

Bhola realized the bandits were beginning to lose hope of finding him and his friends in the crowd. They looked like they were trying to leave.

'Oh no! The police aren't here yet, so I must stop the robbers somehow; they can't leave yet!' thought Bhola.

He looked around desperately, until he saw one of the Choliya dancers taking a break from the procession. He was resting with his back against a shop window. His long, colourful skirt swept the ground behind him and his painted eyebrows shot up as Bhola approached him.

'May I please speak with you?' he asked. 'My friends and I are in trouble and we need your help!'

'Are you all right, son?' the dancer asked, worried.

Bhola signalled for him to come closer and told him about the entire incident with the bandits, pointing them out in the crowd. They had managed to make their way towards the edge of the crowd, Bhola realized in panic.

'Don't worry, we will stop them, come what may,' the Choliya dancer said. 'You stand up on this wall and guide

us!' he said, as he shot through the crowd like lightning.

As he joined the fierce dancing circles, swords and shields clanged against each other and the entire circle of dancers moved rapidly towards the edge of the crowd—just as Bhola pointed them in the right direction.

Before he knew it, the Choliyas had encircled the bandits within their dancing circle, making it impossible for them to leave. Each time one of the four bandits tried to approach the edge of the circle to escape, the dancers would jab their swords towards them, scaring them off.

'They are trapped! It worked!' Bhola squealed from the top of the wall.

Just then he saw Bhaguni in the crowd, leading six policemen towards the Choliyas.

'Over here!' he shouted with all his might. Bhaguni saw him and he directed the policemen towards the bandits.

The Choliyas let the policemen inside the circle who arrested the thieves. By this time, the audience had gathered around the Choliyas and cheered loudly when the thieves were caught.

'What a dramatic finale!' someone shouted, as they saw the thieves being led away by the policemen.

'I'll say, this was a Holi to remember,' Bhola said to Bhaguni and Kanu, as they prepared to leave for their homes. 'The Choliya dancers did, in a way, get rid of evil, didn't they?' Bhola wondered out aloud as Bhaguni and Kanu smiled.

'By the way, I hope you finally found your drinking water,' Bhola asked, looking towards Bhaguni.

'Yes, silly you,' said Bhaguni. 'I did, and it looks like you finally found your courage too,' she giggled, and the sound of tinkling bells filled the air yet again.

16.
Pilgrimage

The dusty, winding road from Dehradun to Rishikesh was making little Gehni dizzy. The narrow road along the mountains was steep and the bus would jerk each time they would approach a bend in the road, which was once in every three minutes or so.

She felt the food do summersaults in her stomach, wanting to jump out of her throat each time the bus swivelled sharply.

'I hope this pilgrimage is worth all this trouble,' she thought, as she forced her eyes shut and rested her head on the seat, next to her mother.

She hadn't wanted to go on this journey in the first place, but her parents convinced her that visiting this temple in Rishikesh would be a one-of-a-kind experience. She would be blessed with good health, a good school record and excellent wealth in the future, they promised.

'But you said, God is everywhere. Then why do we have to go all the way to Rishikesh to pray? You know how much I hate travelling uphill. It just makes me ill!' Gehni had argued earlier.

'What is the purpose of this pilgrimage?' she asked.

'Places of worship have a beautiful, calming effect on us. They bring us peace, and that brings us closer to God,' Mother had said, trying to calm her down.

When Gehni opened her eyes next, they were already at the Rishikesh bus stand. People were unloading their bags and jostling to get out of the bus. If they wanted to make it to the temple by 11:00 a.m., they had to rush.

Soon, the family found themselves thrust out of the bus and pushed along their way to the temple, with hundreds of other devotees.

The devotees chanted and prayed fervently on their steep climb across a hillock to visit the famous shrine that promised to grant their wishes, no matter how impossible they were. Little wonder then, the temple saw thousands of visitors every day.

Gehni and her parents were trudging along the temple path when they befriended another family of three—a particularly loud lady, along with a gentleman whose expression looked like he was always pleasantly surprised and their son, a quiet little boy. The boy didn't seem to be interested in speaking to anyone, so Gehni left him alone.

The new family offered them biscuits and nuts, home-made snacks, jam and biscuits along the way.

'We have come to pray for our son,' the father of the boy managed to say, his mouth full of laddoos (an Indian sweet).

'My wife says coming here to pray will ensure that our son's problem will be solved,' he said, trying to accommodate another laddoo in his mouth.

Gehni and her parents looked at the young boy who looked perfectly fine to them.

'What about you?' asked the lady, directing her question to Gehni's mother.

'Are you here to ask for something specific?'

'Uh, not really,' Gehni's mother replied, a bit flustered, still wondering about the boy. 'We are just here for the lovely...'

'Actually the problem is...' the loud lady cut off Gehni's mother.

'Our son is...well, he doesn't speak at all. He doesn't laugh with us, doesn't share stories like other children do with their parents,' she shrugged.

'The doctors say his speech and hearing are fine but...' she shrugged again. 'We just don't know what's wrong with him.'

Gehni heard the boy sigh sharply and look away.

His mother leaned closer and whispered dramatically, loud enough for everyone to hear, 'We think, perhaps he's possessed.'

Gehni and her parents shot another secretive glance at the little boy. They found his mother's statement hard to believe. Frail and tall with a faraway look in his eyes, even though the boy was a stark contrast to his loud mother and snack-chomping father, he didn't seem odd at all.

After an hour of climbing upwards, they reached the

top of the hillock which was buzzing with the crowd of devotees. Exhausted, the two families decided to sit down at the waiting area of the temple just to catch their breath.

SWOOOSH!

Cough. Cough. Cough.

The boy's mother went into a coughing bout.

Standing directly above her on the edge of the temple's top floor was a bare-boned old man, broom in his hand, trembling.

The boy and his mother were both covered in dust from the man's broom.

'What is the matter with you?' cried the boy's father, looking up at the sweeper. 'Have you no sense?'

The old man walked downstairs, kept the broom aside and folded his hands together, indicating he was sorry.

'I don't want your stupid apology!' the loud woman yelled at the top of her voice. 'You stupid, stupid man... are we supposed to visit the temple now, like this...dirty and disgusting?'

A small crowd was starting to gather around them, curious to see what the ruckus was about.

'Open your mouth and say something, foolish man!' the boy's father was furious. He had even stopped munching.

The old man simply bowed, eyes lowered. He picked up his broom and turned away and started to sweep the other side of the temple.

'What an arrogant old man!' cried the mother of the boy. 'Look how he simply walked away after insulting us!' She appealed to the gathering crowds, looking for sympathy.

In the meantime, the crowd also started asking questions.

'Who is that arrogant, rude man anyway?' someone asked.

'He should be asked to leave the temple, if this is the way he behaves with devotees!' someone else said.

'Perhaps he's here simply to insult us devotees!' a third voice said.

The crowd was starting to get out of hand when Gehni's father stepped in.

'Please calm down, people. It seemed like an honest mistake and it's only an old sweeper. Please leave him alone,' he said, managing to control the gathering.

They looked at the sweeper who, as if in a trance, had continued sweeping the temple floor, his back bent low and his head lowered.

'He hasn't even reacted to all this uproar about him,' Gehni's mother observed.

Gehni, on the other hand, was observing the little boy, who couldn't take his eyes off the old sweeper. Gehni thought she saw him blinking back tears in his eyes.

As the crowd slowly dispersed, the two families jostled their way into the long queue at the main entrance of the temple.

The scene was bursting with colour—strings of saffron marigold flowers filled baskets woven from brown dried leaves, yellow and vermillion powder stained the foreheads of ascetics sitting cross-legged on street corners, and the deep blue of the sunny winter sky, with the fresh whites of the priestly garments, melded together to form a vibrant moving picture.

Gehni took it all in with a smile. Until suddenly, she stopped in her tracks, eyes straight in front of her.

'The little boy!' Gehni cried out loud. 'He's gone!'

His mother whipped around to find that her son was nowhere to be seen. It seemed like he had disappeared into thin air.

'He was here just a minute ago!' screamed the woman.

'Let's split up and look for him!' Gehni's father said. He divided the group and sent everyone in different directions. The boy's father was too shocked to react.

'Gehni, you stay right here, wait for us until we come back. We will all report here again within twenty minutes,' her father instructed her before hurrying away to look for the boy.

After fifteen minutes of waiting at the same spot, Gehni began to feel restless and irritable. Her feet hurt and all she could think of was finding a place to sit down.

She stepped out of the queue and headed towards the waiting area where the two families had been seated earlier.

As she neared the steps to sit, she saw something that made her jaw drop. The little boy was there—mopping the floor with the same old sweeper!

The boy was kneeling down, scrubbing the waiting area of the temple floor, wringing the coarse cloth dry over the bucket of water next to him and mopping again. The old sweeper was pointing out spots and corners for the boy to sweep, and the boy was obeying, with a smile on his face.

Even as Gehni stared open-mouthed at the scene, she was joined by her parents and then the boy's parents, who had come back from their search, worried and exhausted.

Upon spotting his son, his father cried out, 'Aye Paras! Come here!'

His mother was frantic too. 'Paras! What are you doing there on the filthy floor? Come back at once!'

Paras heard his parents and hurried over to them.

'Yes, Mother, Father. I'm sorry I had to dart out like that. But I just wanted to see the old sweeper again.'

His parents stared at him as he spoke.

They had never heard their son speak so fluently before. Were their prayers answered by coming to this temple?

'See there, that old sweeper—the same one who had mistakenly swept dust over us, he's teaching me how to mop the temple floors!' said the boy, his eyes twinkling.

'What nonsense is this!' cried his mother. 'First, he insults us and then he makes my son do menial jobs for him! Who does he think he is?'

'No, Mother! I requested him to let me assist him.'

'Why on Earth would you do that?' asked his father, still shocked.

'To learn the true meaning of worship, Father!' exclaimed the boy.

'What? Did the sweeper tell you all this, just to make you do his job?' asked his mother.

'No, he's deaf and mute, Mother. Just like you thought I was. The truth is, I like to observe more and speak less, that's all. Just because I am not like you, does not mean something is wrong with me!' he said, as his parents looked at each other.

'I have been observing this man. He does his job of sweeping and mopping the temple floors—the same temple floors that are littered and made filthy by devotees like us,' he said.

Gehni and her parents, for the first time, realized they had been doing the same thing without realizing how much filth they had made.

'If it wasn't for this old man, this temple would not get the respect it receives. So then, isn't his job even more important than that of the priest? Isn't his devotion deeper than that of any devotee?' he asked.

'Yes, he deserves the utmost respect,' Gehni chimed in. 'His work is his worship and I would like to join you in helping him,' she said, as she went over to the sweeper and the boy, picked up another mop cloth and dunked it in the bucket.

The two families looked at each other dumbfounded, and without a word, instead of joining the queue for a glimpse of the holy shrine inside, decided to help the three to mop the temple floors.

As Gehni boarded the bus back home to Dehradun that evening, she knew the purpose of her pilgrimage had been fulfilled.

17.
Postcard

My grandfather's bicycle always struck me as a very odd object. It was big, strong and sturdy enough to ride along the steep and rough mountains, but it was also the most uncomfortable ride in the world. It was painted black, so I always called it, the Black Elephant.

I would stare at it in awe every time Bubu (grandfather) rushed out of the house, sliding it off its heavy stand on which it rested, when parked. He would always urge me to hurry up after him. He would tilt the bicycle sideways towards me, so I could prop myself on the carrier behind him and sit on the makeshift seat.

The bicycle endured the bumps and slippery gravel along the narrow lanes of Mussoorie, as Bubu navigated the sharp bends effortlessly.

The aroma of burning coal fire and boiling rice melted into the air when we cycled through the edge of the village, but it quickly changed into a strong, woody musk as the bicycle glided into the pine forest. Even if I closed my eyes, I could tell where we were passing through, just from what I smelled.

Each time the tyres went over a bump, I would grab on to Bubu's torso, his old checked shirt giving me a whiff of strong detergent.

I would try to distract myself from the poking edges of the bicycle carrier by looking up at the thick canopy of pine trees, evergreen and strong. It was always reassuring to look at these trees, which were about half a century old but still sturdy. They looked like they would probably be the same, half a century later.

'Mahout of the Black Elephant, overlord of mountain shortcuts and warrior of goat traffic,' I would tease him, as I hopped off the carrier, my backside sore and my bones rattling.

I always made it to school on time, no matter how many songs we sang on this journey or how many stops we made to pick wild berries along the way.

He would chuckle and say, 'I'll be back at 1500 hours,' every time he dropped me at the school gate.

And he was always punctual. Even at home, my grandfather would be methodical and disciplined, a remnant from his days as a sailor.

I would pester him for stories every night, and his tales would often spill well beyond bedtime. But once he started recollecting his childhood days, he would forget about the curfews.

He would often tell me about how he and his little

gang of village urchins used to explore the mountainside barefoot, identify birdsongs from across the hills and dig up freshwater springs straight out of the ground, whenever they were thirsty. He ended these stories with an anecdote about a broken bone or two.

Bubu and I had lived together for as long as I could remember. He took me to the village fair every Diwali and I read him letters that came from his naval friends. The sweet and sticky, black-coloured bal mithai was the one common love we shared, and every Saturday after school, Bubu had a plate waiting for me.

On one such Saturday, when I rushed out of my class to greet Bubu at the school gate at three o'clock sharp, I was surprised to find that he wasn't there. I walked around to the back gate of the school to look for him but couldn't find him there either.

I waited for more than two hours under a tree near the gate—the same one he would usually lean his bicycle against. As the crowd thinned and the chatter of students died down, I kept my eyes firmly on the gate, hoping to catch a glimpse of my grandfather. He had never missed a day, except when his cow went into labour one day exactly at 2:45 p.m., delivering a beautiful baby calf two hours later.

But that was an exception. He didn't even have animals any more, so I wondered what could have possibly kept him from coming to school to fetch me.

Tired and irritated, I walked out of the school gate myself, dragging my schoolbag behind me. It would take me at least an hour and fifteen minutes to walk home, I calculated.

By the time I was halfway home, I was completely out of breath. It would start getting dark in an hour, I thought, as I picked up pace, despite my aching limbs and thumping heart.

As soon as I reached the final bend around the road, my heart suddenly sank. I saw my grandfather's bicycle lying sideways on the edge of the road, its hind tyre spinning in a tizzy. My mouth went dry.

I tried to choke back tears, expecting signs of a possible accident. I took a few steps around the bend to look over the edge, into the steep valley below.

I turned cold. He wouldn't have survived if he had fallen off the bend.

Just then, I heard footsteps echoing in the distance. I followed the sound to see my grandfather walking in the direction of our home, with his back towards me.

'Bubu!' I screamed as loudly as I could, my voice rumbling. 'Over here!'

He didn't turn, so I raced ahead to catch up, my heart thumping.

'Oh! Chotu, you're here!' he said, as he turned around to see me. 'Good heavens, I have lost my way! I...I can't tell if it's this way or that,' he tried to explain but couldn't complete the sentence.

'What?' I was aghast. 'Bubu, you forgot the way to my school?' I asked, shocked. We had taken the same route for the past eight years, every day.

'I don't know, I just don't know...,' he mumbled under his breath. 'School? Are you coming back from school now? Why didn't you wait till I picked you up?'

I held his hand and led him to his bicycle, a strange feeling washing over me.

I wanted to tell him he was meant to pick me up two hours ago. I wanted to ask him how he managed to forget the way to my school. Maybe he had some work to do and he was simply pretending to hide the fact that he had forgotten to pick me up from school. I wanted to be angry.

Instead, I was frightened. And sad. 'Something is wrong with him,' I thought.

As I sat on the small seat behind him, navigating the rest of the way home, I realized he had been forgetting small things for the last few months. I just hadn't noticed.

In the past few months, he had complained that he had trouble calculating the change he got from the vegetable vendors. 'I don't remember where I have kept my socks,' he had exclaimed one morning. He had even left his bed unmade a few times, which for a former sailor in the Navy, was nothing short of a crime.

That evening, I was hesitant to let him go alone on his daily trip to the vegetable market, so I accompanied him on his walk.

I walked one step behind him, watching his heavy-set frame slouch slightly, and his shoulders droop downwards. I followed him to the local shop in the market.

'Two litres of milk, one kilo ghee and one kilo... one kilo...uh, I...I...I don't know what I came here for,' Bubu mumbled, rubbing his forehead. His face was flushed red.

'And a dozen eggs,' I chimed in.

'Oh yes, eggs...uh...probably eggs,' said Bubu, a look of confusion sweeping across his face. He thrust a few notes into my palm to give to the shopkeeper and stepped out in a hurry.

When I followed him outside, trying to juggle the items in my hand, Bubu turned towards me, 'I don't know what's happening to me, bal. It's not normal...this is not normal. I just forgot what I came to buy,' he said, his voice trembling while he spoke. 'I was never this forgetful and...confused... something is wrong with me, I think.'

He rested his hand on my shoulder as he stepped onto the sidewalk and sat on the bench, facing the sun setting between the mountains.

'It's getting blurry,' Bubu said, looking into the distance. 'Everything is blurry because of the fog, ha?'

'Don't worry, Bubu, we will be home safely,' I reassured him, even though there was no fog that evening. Perhaps Bubu's vision was failing too.

The next day, I went to the village chief's house to inform him of my grandfather's condition and perhaps get some advice on what I should do next.

'Probably just old age, boy, don't worry,' the chief said, while examining his vegetable patch in his backyard.

'You see these leaves, they get old and yellowed with age,' he was wielding a pair of scissors in one hand and holding a bunch of yellowing leaves in another.

SNIP.

'They must go when they have to, boy. Do you understand?' he asked, as I nodded, even though I didn't understand.

'New leaves will come in its place. It's simply the law of nature,' the chief said, peering at me over his glasses that rested on the edge of his pointed nose.

SNIP, SNIP.

Was he talking about Bubu? Yes, I knew he was old and would die someday, but I loved him, and I simply could not imagine what would happen to me if he went. We had only each other as family.

I walked home, angry and sad. 'How could the chief have been so casual? It wasn't his loved one who was suffering, I guess, so he didn't care,' I thought, as hot tears rolled down my cheeks.

'Oh, why Bubu? Why me? Why us?'

I stopped to sit on a lone bench by the road, sobbing till I thought my heart would burst.

By the time I reached home that evening, the postman was at the doorway, arguing with Bubu.

'But it is addressed to you!' the postman was saying to Bubu.

Bubu was shaking his head vigorously. 'I don't know a Bisht. This has been wrongly addressed!'

When I reached the doorway, the postman thrust the postcard into my palm.

'The old man is losing it,' he said, walking away.

As I looked at the sender's name, I realized who it was. As we sat down for dinner, I placed the postcard in front of Bubu.

'You remember Bisht?' I asked.

'Oh for god's sake! The postman kept asking me this, and now you. I don't know anyone by this name. There has been some mistake!'

'Bubu, Bisht has been your friend for the past thirty years. You were in the naval training academy together,' I gulped, trying to swallow the big lump building in my throat.

'You have told me so many stories about him, Bubu,' I said quietly. 'You forgot him?' I asked.

'Would he forget me too?' I thought, nervously.

Just before bedtime, I decided to open the envelope addressed to Bubu. Inside was a postcard from erstwhile Bombay. It was a picture of a ship docked in a yard and a flock of seagull flying above it.

Behind the postcard was a message that read, 'Nautiyal, old chap. Enjoy the present moment. It's all we really have.'

I could barely sleep that night. What did it mean?

Early next morning, even before the sun rose in the sky, I rushed to Bubu's room to wake him up.

'Wake up, Bubu! We have to go,' I said, shaking him out of bed.

Bubu mumbled something sleepily but thankfully didn't ask questions as he followed me outside the house. I threw him a sweater and said, 'Bubu, let's take the Black Elephant out for a spin. It's been a while, hasn't it?'

'But, Nayan, you know very well I have been asked not to ride the bicycle anymore, especially after that day when I got lost on the way to your school,' he said, his face grim. 'The villagers have advised...'

'Bubu, please. Do it for me!' I pleaded. I knew he couldn't argue with that.

I hopped on behind him. Bubu was excited to be riding the metallic beast again and it gave him a fresh burst of energy. He pedaled quickly, and we glided through the pine forest, going farther inside than we had ever ventured before.

'Where are you guiding me, bal?' asked Bubu with a smile, as the cool morning breeze swept across his face. I knew he didn't actually care where we were going. He was simply enjoying the ride.

'Just keep going straight, Bubu,' I said, pretending to have a plan.

As soon as we reached the small mountain bend, I asked Bubu to park the bike against an old pine tree. I got off the carrier seat, my backside sore from the ride.

'This way,' I said, as I led him across the hillside. 'Oh, but let's take our slippers off, first!'

Bubu grinned and nodded, as he loved walking barefoot on the soft mud. He would do so as a child, and I knew that only because of his many bedtime stories.

We walked up the mountain, picking wild berries along the way—some of whose names Bubu remembered and some of which I recollected from his childhood tales.

He stopped in his tracks suddenly, only to hush me into silence. A bird was humming in the distance. 'The blue whistling thrush,' he whispered, triumphantly. 'It only whistles at dawn and dusk, like a sleep-time and wake-up call.'

We walked for a long time until the sun was overhead, relishing the sweet-and-sour colourful berries along the way until we realized we were thirsty.

Bubu smiled, dropped to his knees and to my bewilderment, started digging the soft mud out beneath him. He dug furiously and let out a squeal when a fresh, cold fountain of water sprouted out of the ground, exactly like in his childhood story!

He chuckled as he gestured for me to drink the water. It was the sweetest water I had ever tasted.

On our way back home on the bicycle, I hugged Bubu to shield myself against the cold, evening wind, the whiff of that familiar detergent filling my senses once again. Then, he said something I would never forget.

'Bal, I don't know how many days I have left and I can barely remember the past, but I can tell you that today was the best day of my life.'

I nodded and smiled, thinking of the postcard and thanking his old friend silently.

From that day on, Bubu and I shared many of these 'best days', until he passed away, exactly one year later.

I wasn't sad anymore. I wasn't scared or angry either. Instead, I was happy because together, my Bubu and I had the time of our lives, every single day.